Shattered Tomorrows

C.L. Kraemer

Credits
Cover Artist: Genene Valleau
Editor: Shawneen Staley

Printed in the United States of America

WHAT THEY ARE SAYING ABOUT
Shattered Tomorrows

This book made me crazy, yet I loved it! The story sucked me into the action from the first page and I watched it unfold with each Chapter. I'm a Salemite but too young to have been out in the clubs at that time. However, I don't remember hearing this story, and Ms. Kraemer's tale sent me to older friends who were at the Oregon Museum Tavern the night of the event.

Lucy Daniels has her life all set until Gregg Halstrom shows up. Tall and good-looking, he fits the picture of the "perfect" Prince Charming. Lucy fights falling for this handsome bartender but finds her heart being swept away with his caring and sensitivity. She's quickly heading toward love. Add to this mix, a brooding figure hovering in the background monitoring Lucy's every move. Dubbed "The Strange One" by the bartenders and waitresses of the clubs he enters, Richard White has made it his mission in life to protect the woman he fancies--Lucy Daniels.

Because of Richard's maniacal devotion to Lucy, many around her will be in danger.

The author states this is a fiction novel based loosely on facts but I have to wonder, what part was fiction and what part is fact?

I would recommend this to anyone that enjoys mystery and true crime literature as Shattered Tomorrows is well written and a worthy addition to any book collection.

Once again Ms. Kraemer delivers a story deserving of five Angel Wings.

Angel Eyes Reviews
Reviewer – Lori N.

Dedication

In memory of the four lost and twenty wounded,
we won't forget.

Chapter One

Staring at the reflective elevator door, I didn't recognize the middle-aged face staring back at me.

When had I grown so old? When had gray become the dominant color of my dark brown hair? And please, tell me, where the hell had I picked up those doggie jowls?

Cassie Thorpe, my best friend since, well, what seemed forever, looked into the reflection.

"What are you doing?" She cocked her head in that funny way she always does when she's questioning my sanity. This time she added crossed arms and a hitched eyebrow.

"Wondering how age snuck up and attacked me without my knowledge." I peered at my likeness, my finger tracing a line from my nose to my chin around what used to be a full voluptuous mouth.

"Oh, God."

I watched Cassie roll her eyes as she uncrossed her arms and adjusted the purse on her shoulder. She shook her head and blew air between her lips.

"Lucy, just schedule a face lift. I told you I'd front you the money."

The elevator had reached the top floor of the Equitable Building in downtown Salem. The interior had recently undergone a major renovation and featured Italian marble in most of the lobby and down the hallways. Small areas of plush carpet covered the remainder of the floor. The new owners had muted the government gray walls with a faux Tuscan-inspired paint, adding art deco sconces to the walls. Bronze lamps hung from the cathedral ceiling adding a touch of elegance to the lobby area. Dark leather couches and chairs placed in comfortable conversation settings invited the visitor to stop and admire the effect. Every effort had been made to rid the visitor of the government feel of the square, granite and smoked-glass building.

"Where are we going again?" I followed Cassie out of the lift toward a hallway that wound to sculpted, cherry-stained office doors bearing the gold suite number.

She placed a hand on the gold-plated door handle and turned as she spoke to me. "My lawyer. Bobby's balking about handing over the chalet at Mt. Bachelor."

"Oh."

We entered an office painted in muted tones of blue. The money invested in the cherry wood desk occupied by the receptionist would've paid for that facelift Cassie had offered. The blue-gray guest couches were satiny soft and comfortable.

Speaking into her silver, state-of-the-art headset, the pencil-thin blonde at the desk announced Cassie.

I hadn't even transferred the latest issue of People magazine to my lap when a door, magnificently blended into the cool blue wall opened revealing a young man wearing a fitted, black Baroni suit. A Rolex peeked from beneath the sleeve of a silk dress shirt and Gucci loafers covered his feet. He lifted a manicured finger and beckoned us into the inner sanctum.

I would've been happy to stay and read the most recent dirt on the latest *it* couple, but Cassie dragged me behind her. My feet sank into the carpet. I swear. It was like walking on that miracle foam bedding. I turned to see if I'd left my footprints. Cassie cleared her throat and shook her head.

I shrugged my shoulders and stood awkwardly, waiting for permission to seat myself.

The young man moved around the L-shaped desk made of Koa wood and seated himself in a large steel-blue leather chair. He motioned us to sit in the two upholstered chairs in front of his monstrosity of a desk as he perched straight backed and rigid in the chair. Behind him an impressive ten foot tall, thirty foot long array of silver gray curtains waved slightly with the breeze from the rising warmth of the heater.

Once we were all settled and our roles firmly established, he moved to the front of his desk to languidly lean on the edge. Grasping Cassie's hand, he placed a delicate kiss on the top of it, his steely eyes gazing into her chocolate brown ones.

"What can *I*… do for *you*?"

Cassie pulled a deep, shuddering breath in and blew out slowly.

"Donald, I hope you don't mind if my best friend Lucy sits in on this." She batted her eyes at him. "I think I'll need her before we're done."

Donald, I guessed that was his name, nodded his head so slightly at me I wasn't sure if I was being acknowledged or if he was flexing his neck muscles.

"Ma'am."

Okay. That's it; I've had enough. No one condescends to me. I don't have to take this.

I started to rise but stopped halfway up when Cassie laid a hand on my arm.

"Lucy, please? For me?"

What I do for my friends… I sat back down and folded my arms. *This had better be good.*

I watched my friend morph before my very eyes. Her shoulders sagged, bottom lip took on a quivering life of its own, and she again sucked a deep ragged breath into her lungs.

"It's Robert."

I lifted my left eyebrow. I'd *never* heard Cassie use her ex-husband's proper name.

The young barrister leaned closer, concentrating all his attention on my well-endowed, and rich, friend.

"What has he done now, Cassandra?"

3

I choked, feigning a cough. If I'd called her Cassandra, I'd have worn the impression of her knuckles on my bicep for two weeks.

"I... I... I just can't take it." Cassie picked up her purse from the floor and pulled out a lace-edged hanky which she dabbed to the inside corner of her right eye.

I sat with my mouth gaping. I'd seen this delicate flower drag a 6' 2", *drunk*, rugby player to the front of the bar where we'd both worked at the time and THROW him into the parking lot--by herself.

The person sitting next to me now was nobody *I* knew.

Donald leaned over and murmured just low enough I nearly missed it. "I know just what to do."

He gave a curt nod of his head and stood.

I panicked. There was *no way* I wanted to be witness to fooling around, even if she was my best friend.

Donald turned from the desk to the wall of fabric behind him. Picking up a remote control from the desktop, he pointed it at the curtains. Slowly they slid toward the corners, revealing a wall of glass from ceiling to the floor.

It was at that moment I must have lost my mind.

Outside the sky was pewter-toned with horizon-to-horizon clouds pelting fat raindrops to the ground. Tiny rivulets ran down the outside of the glass wall. Even with the gloom of the rain, natural light from the sky brightened the space overpowering the subtle glow of the lamps in the room.

Donald turned to face Cassie and took his place in the leather captain's chair behind the desk.

"There. That should help. Now tell me everything that's happening."

Cassie launched into a diatribe about Bobby and his girlfriend, now his wife, and droned on and on.

It all faded to so much background noise. Something about the act of revealing the floor to ceiling windows set off a trigger in my mind.

4

The cloud-filled sky faded to darkness and city lights twinkled in the distance. I felt a thump, thump, thumping in my chest and vague strains of a Donna Summer song echoed somewhere in the distance. Tracer lights tracked around the floor which was oak parquet now. Stale beer and cigarettes tickled my nose, and there was a subtle undertone of prime rib tinged with horseradish and baked potatoes. I ran my tongue over my lips in anticipation, the tangy bite of lemon tweaking my taste buds. The thrumming of the disco beat set my heart racing, and I found myself sweating. *Man, it's hot!*

Someone was tugging on my arm. I was not in the mood to deal with amorous drunks tonight. I was going to introduce his face to my tray if he didn't stop tugging on my arm.

"Lucy! Lucy!"

How can this drunk know my name?

"LUCY!"

Light slowly filtered through my fog. The thundering of the music was gone, and the obsidian night sky melted into the dreary, sullen gray of weeping clouds. Gone were the tracer lights on the floor. Carpet now covered the space and the bouquet of prime rib had fled the room. No stale beer. No stale cigarettes.

I glanced up into the worried eyes of my friend Cassie.

"Are you all right? You, like, *went away* for a minute."

I smiled weakly. "Yeah, I'm all right. How about I stop at the ladies' room while you finish up? I'll meet you by the elevators."

"Fine. I'll be done here shortly."

Donald rose from his desk and, coming around the corner, escorted me to the door.

I made a big deal of asking the receptionist to direct me to the little girls' room. It was all for show. I knew where the ladies' room was on this floor and every floor in the building. The new owners may have updated the furnishings, but the layout was still the same. I'd spent more time in these restrooms than I'd wanted.

As I entered, my footsteps echoed on the tile-covered concrete floors, against the tiles on the walls. The air freshener squirted neutralizing spray into the air, eliminating offensive odors.

So-o-o-o-o different from… back then. So different from when a dozen or more drunk, rowdy ladies crowded into a space designed for just four people.

I leaned my head against the cool surface and slowly brought myself back to the present.

I was sure Cassie was going to ask me about my mental vacation. She was just young enough, she'd not been clubbing around the time I was recalling. She would not remember this place or the Incident that made international news.

"You okay?" Cassie poked her head around the concrete dividing wall.

I looked at the worried brown eyes searching my face. She and I had been through a lot in the years we'd known each other. But even good friends had secrets from one another, right?

"Lucy, what the hell is going on? You're scaring me. Come on, you can confide in me. We are best buds, aren't we?"

I looked into the frightened eyes of my best friend. *Can I really tell her everything? Will we still be best friends when she finds out I was responsible for the deaths of four people?*

Chapter Two

Common sense took over. I pulled myself from the wall and moved to the sink, grabbing a dampened paper towel and placing it against my forehead.

"Just feeling a little woozy. Guess I'm hungrier than I realized. What say we go to the Salem Centre Mall and get something from the food court?"

I attempted a weak smile.

"Like hell. We're going to The Block, and you're going to eat a proper sandwich while I drink my lunch, after which you'll drive me home. You scared the hell out of me."

She waited until I tossed the paper towel in the trash then linked her arm through mine. We emerged from the restroom and strode toward the elevators. An appropriately muted bell tone announced the arrival of the moving room. We entered the empty compartment and leaned against the back wall of the car. On the way down, I couldn't even look at my own reflection in the polished steel wall. I'd done a pretty good job of hiding from the thirty-year-old memories to this point. With the exception of the action in the lawyer's office, I hadn't experienced any *little vacations* since, well, *that* time. Don't get me wrong… I'd tried counseling. But after a short amount of time, one begins to realize the counselors consider the whole world crazy. It was not successful.

We stood for a moment in the lobby observing people going about their business. Cassie, thanks to Bobby's excellent investments and a good, actually great, divorce lawyer, was independently wealthy. She didn't work; she served on committees. I, on the other hand, was working two jobs and finishing my college.

"Cass, I really need to get back to the office." I attempted my best pleading-eye-look on her.

"Nope. I contacted Gordon... "

My boss.

"... before the meeting and you're mine for the next couple of days. I guaranteed him the contract on my next home. Oh, yes. I also called Bill at the Lounge and made a deal with him to bring the members of my committee to the bar after the next meeting. He was skeptical at first, but when I personally guaranteed him two nights worth a thousand dollars, he agreed to find someone to work your shifts. "

"Great. Gee, everyone makes out but me, Cassie. Remember? I've bills to pay and classes to attend."

She turned to me and started the lip-quivering act. Real tears pooled in her eyes.

"Lucy, please?"

"Fine, but if I have to take my classes over because I flunked them, you're paying for it."

I watched as a smirk touched the corners of her mouth. Score one for Cassie.

"I'll cover what you're losing in wages and tips. Just remind me on Sunday."

"Count on it, girlfriend."

As the receptionist, bookkeeper and gofer for a landscaping business, I kept track of one hundred workers at any number of jobs on a continuous basis. Friday and Saturday nights, I bartended at a little place called The Touchdown Lounge. Monday through Thursday nights, I drove to Western Oregon University to finish my teaching degree. When I was done, I'd have a year of on-the-job training, then hopefully, a classroom of my own. Until then free time was as elusive as single, straight men near my age.

Cassie and I stood under the awning of the Equitable building waiting for the light on our side of Center Street to turn green. We dashed across the street and went into the department store which had been there as long as I could remember. New signs had appeared in the street windows announcing their going-out-of-business sale. Another dinosaur bites the dust.

I started toward the food court. Cassie grasped my elbow, steering me in the direction of the parking lot.

"The Block."

She wasn't going to let me deter her. I sighed and gave in. Like I said, I've seen what she can do to a 250-pound rugby player... I was no match.

When we pulled up and snagged a parking spot in front of the pub-- no easy feat on a normal day--I held out an inkling of hope it was too early for them to be open.

"Darn. They're still closed."

Cassie shot me a withering look.

"No. They opened half an hour ago. Trust me, I know."

I wasn't about to ask how, so resigned myself to eating while Cassie paid and drank the afternoon away.

I hadn't wiled away an afternoon like this since... well, since the year of the Incident.

Don't get me wrong. I used to party hardy, but one too many mornings waking up with an anvil pounding in my head curbed my party-girl days.

My friends loved it. I still partied, but without the alcohol. They scored with a party buddy and designated driver rolled into one--a winning combination.

Cassie locked the car; the familiar chirp announcing success then tossed me the keys.

We wandered inside and picked a table that afforded a view of the street. We hadn't quite settled in our seats when a tall Bloody Mary was placed in front of Cassie. Her face lit up.

"Mary! You're a life saver."

"What about your friend?" the waitress raised a perfectly plucked brow.

"Raspberry ice tea, if you have it." I grabbed the menu.

"Coming up."

Cassie started in on Bobby's latest screw up, going on about his new bimbo wife and how she'd become pregnant to make sure he stayed around.

I decided to have a California club sandwich; fancy name for a club sandwich with avocados. Gives the restaurant the right to charge an extra $2.00. I'd just caught the tail end of her rant.

"Oh, so Bobby's going to be a dad?"

Cassie had just opened her mouth to start in on some other imagined sin and sat glaring at me, mouth gaping.

"Don't tell me you're happy for him." She furrowed her brows, causing a small wrinkle to form on her forehead.

I rolled my eyes.

The waitress picked that fortuitous moment to bring my drink.

"Here you go; raspberry ice tea, as ordered. Are you ready to order?"

"Yeah. I'd like the California Club on sourdough, please."

She was writing furiously. She turned to Cassie. "Anything else?"

Cassie tossed her hair behind her shoulder. "Nope."

Mary bounced off to the kitchen as I replaced the menu in the holder. "Well?"

I looked up to find Cassie trying to glare a hole through me.

"Well, what?"

"Are you *happy* Bobby's going to be a father?"

Now this sounds like a simply put question. It wasn't. It was a trick question. I was beginning to understand how husbands felt. There was no winning answer.

"I just think it's interesting."

"Interesting!" Cassie's voice was rising in volume and pitch. "Why is that?"

"After all those years of telling you he didn't want kids, and now this."

I shrugged my shoulders.

"Interesting."

She sat for a moment, stirring her bloody Mary. Then she took a deep draught from the straw, rolled the liquid around her mouth and swallowed. She was very subdued when she next spoke.

"You're right… interesting."

"Cassie?"

"Hmm?"

"Do you really want the chalet in Bend?" I watched her bristle. Her mouth became a straight line and she sat stiffly in her chair.

"Why, Lucy?"

"Frankly, I can't remember the last time you went over the mountains."

"Yeah, but I might…"

"Cassie."

She took a deep swig from the container in front of her, slurping all the liquid from the glass. She turned, nodded at Mary then crossed her arms.

"What?"

"You hate the thought of running into Bobby. Admit it."

"What will you do when it snows? Where are you going to go out? You hate country western music. You told me yourself the only thing you ever did when you and Bobby used to go skiing was sit in the bar and drink hot toddies. Doesn't sound fun to me."

I reached over and put my hand on her arm. She tried to jerk away, but I held tight.

"You are only hanging on to the chalet because you want what Bobby has."

She yanked the napkin holder to her and grabbed a handful. She blew her nose, swiped at the tears pooling in her eyes thrashing her mascara, and took a deep swig of the new drink in front of her.

"So what's your point?"

She looked at me through teary, smudged lashes.

"Give Bobby the chalet."

"No wa…"

"Listen to me. Bobby's business has pretty much moved to the Bend area, right? With him, the wife and baby in Bend, you'll never see them. If you hate seeing him, then why would you hold on to a vacation home that increases your chances of running into him? Give it up and cut the ties."

I wasn't sure if she'd been listening but the sniffling stopped and her frown was melting. Her pout turned to a pensive, considering look.

"Just think about it.

Chapter Three

We sat at The Block for the rest of the afternoon--Cassie getting thoroughly soused and me wondering if my kidneys would ever forgive me for dumping so much tea on them.

After driving her home and putting her to bed, I called my boss.

"Listen, Gordon…"

"Lucy. Stop. You deserved the time off. While I didn't get along as well before I hired you, we did manage to run our business for, what, 25 years? I'll see you on Monday. Just don't call out sick or I'll come hunt you down."

"You have my word on that."

"Good. Have a great weekend, Lucy."

"You, too, Gordon."

Now what was I going to do? I hadn't signed up for any Friday classes this quarter, and I was skipping my Thursday class for my going-out buddy who was presently at home passed out.

I wandered around my house. It was too quiet. Where *was* Tessa? My lab mix hadn't come out to greet me. I'd fix that. I moseyed into the kitchen and opened the cabinet under the 1950's style oven. Pulling out the bag of dog food, I made no effort to silence the noise. Within two minutes, I heard the tick, tick, tick of nails on hardwood floors.

I looked at my thirty-pound mutt as she dashed up to me. Filling her bowl with food, I stepped back, not wanting to be run over. I put the bag back in the cupboard and turned to find two quizzical dark brown eyes peering at me.

"What, baby?"

She stepped toward me and looked up.

"Yep, you're right. I'm home early and I'm going to stay home. Go ahead and eat. We'll just curl up on the couch and watch TV. How's that?"

I reached down and passed my hand over her velvety fur, pausing long enough to scratch behind her ears. She began wagging her tail and drifted to her food dish.

I'd had about as much tea as I could handle but was feeling a bit chilled. I started a pot of coffee brewing and moved to the living room. On my way through the dining room, I hesitated then opened the bottom door of the 1940's style, pine hutch my mom had gifted me.

My hand moved of its own accord and grabbed a picture album. Today's little foray into the past left me wanting to make a quick visit down memory lane.

Settling on the couch, I opened the aging photo book. There I was… slim, no bulldog chinline, no bags under the eyes and dark chestnut hair shimmering under the photographer's lights. The lips pouted and the hazel of my eyes popped with the shadow I'd been wearing. I recall the shoot--I slept for all of three hours the previous night and I looked great.

I get eight hours sleep now and people ask if I don't feel well. I sighed and put the album on the coffee table. I could smell the recently brewed java, and being desperately in need, I strolled to the kitchen and filled a mug. I meandered back to the living room. Once settled on the couch, I pulled the album to me. Tessa jumped up, turned three times in place then lay down on my tucked feet. Unconsciously, I ran my hand down her soft coat. She sighed and closed her eyes.

I realized I was putting off the inevitable and flipped the pages to his picture.

There he stood; hair feathered back, liquor bottle in one hand, soda gun in the other. His dark hair set off his blue eyes and the moustache he wore sparkled under the light of the beer signs behind him.

14

He was smiling at the camera, brilliant white teeth flashing and tanned skin accenting his dimples. It was the era of the fitted shirt, and his emphasized the two hours he worked out each day of the week.

My heart ached. It had been nearly ten years since I'd taken a step into the past and looked at this picture. I ran my finger over the face and found my breath catching in my throat. A warm, wet tongue licked a tear I hadn't felt slipping down my cheek.

"Oh, Tessa, I miss him so." I whispered my love to the photo knowing he wouldn't hear me. He couldn't hear me. He couldn't hear anybody.

Chapter Four

Cassie called Saturday morning. Well, early afternoon actually.

"Lucy?" Her voice sounded raw, painful.

"Cassie? What's the matter? You sound like hell."

"I feel like it, too. At first, I thought I was hung over, but apparently, I *acquired* food poisoning from the celery in the Bloody Marys at The Block."

Why did I have the unsettling feeling I was listening to the beginning of a lawsuit? Oh, yeah, I was talking to my sue-happy friend, Cassandra.

"How can you be sure it's food poisoning?"

"Cause I spent Thursday night and all day Friday in the hospital."

This explained the reason her phone kept going to message when I called Friday. I'd been worried, but Cassie had been known to sleep away a day or even just take her phone off the hook for privacy. Popularity had its price.

"Whatever you do, don't get your stomach pumped."

"It's not real high on my list of things to do, Cassie."

"Well, don't ever get to that point."

"I'll try not to. Why are you calling?"

"Even as tipsy as I was Thursday, something about the way you were acting at Donald's office wasn't right. I need to know what's wrong, Lucy. And don't tell me nothing. I know better.

"Pack up Tessa's food and bring her blanket. Then pack yourself up an overnight bag and come out to my house. I'm not going anywhere until Monday. My fridge is filled and the local pizza parlor will deliver. I want to hear what this is all about, and I suspect it's going to take all weekend."

I sighed.

16

"I heard that. You're wasting time. Just get out here."

She hung up without so much as a goodbye, but then that was Cassie. I knew she'd harangue me until I showed up at her doorstep, so I started putting together a small valise.

Tessa stood off to one side of my bed and watched. I picked up the bag and took it to the living room, placing it next to the door. As I suspected, I had a shadow monitoring my every move.

I turned to her. "Would you like to go?"

Ears stood up, eyes popped, and with four paws dancing, my dog pranced around the room.

"I take it that's a yes?"

"Uff."

It was probably the best answer I was going to get. Packing up food bowls and snapping on her leash, we made our way to the company truck I drove. Normally, it stayed in the garage, but my car was still at the Equitable parking garage. I'd have to get it before the end of Sunday or it would be towed.

Tessa settled herself on the passenger's seat and we drove to the neighborhood of mansions on the edge of Silverton.

As I wound my way up the long serpentine driveway, I marveled at Cassie's ability to land on her feet. She really needed to give Bobby the chalet in Bend. If for no other reason than she hated the snow and everything to do with it.

I steered the truck to the entry door and turned off the engine. I wouldn't be blocking anyone as Cassie lived alone and, by her own admission, was going nowhere for the night.

One side of the large entry door opened to feature my best friend wrapped in a blanket and sporting something pink and fuzzy on her feet.

"Need help?"

I couldn't help but giggle. "Just take Tessa inside with you, okay?"

Clutching the blanket tightly around her body, Cassie nodded and shuffled to the passenger side of the truck.

Tessa turned excited circles in the passenger seat.

Cassie opened the door and allowed my 30-pound dog to drag her into the house.

Gathering my overnight things, I followed. I set up Tessa's dishes and settled our things into the room Cassie had designated was ours for the night. We seated ourselves in Cassie's spacious entertainment room overlooking the rolling valley hills.

"Okay, girlfriend. We have alcohol, munchies, and a roaring fire in the fireplace. Spill your guts."

I stared into the dancing yellow and orange flames banked in the fireplace. Pulling in a deep breath I exhaled slowly then took a sip from my margarita. I thought for a moment and plunged in to my story.

"This all started while you were still in Jr. High..."

Chapter Five

Lucy's story

"I came to Salem in 1979 and immediately jumped into the bar scene. I was used to it from where I'd previously lived. Working as a bartender was a great way to make hidden money. I usually met some good-looking guys and could wrangle an invitation or two for a date.

"At that time, the guys were still macho enough to feel they had to buy dinner and drinks to even have the opportunity to make a pass. Women's Lib was still in its infancy here.

I had been working at a nightclub called Heaven."

The doorbell pealed and Cassie held up a finger.

"Pizza. Hot and cooked by someone else."

She disappeared down a long flagstone-lined hallway, appearing ten minutes later with a white flat box that emanated the most delicious smell. On top of the box was a stack of napkins, Parmesan cheese packets and paper plates.

She placed the box in the middle of the coffee table and slowly opened the lid. Waves of garlic scented air wafted through the room. She placed two slices of pizza topped with pepperoni, sausage, linguica and fresh tomatoes on a plate in front of me. Then she filled my margarita glass to the rim.

Completing the same ritual for herself, she settled on the couch and tucked her fuzzy feet beneath her while she bit into the pizza.

"Go on," she mumbled over the tomato pie.

I had just taken a bite myself and was really in no hurry to relate the story she sought. When I'd chewed enough to have room to speak politely, I continued.

"You're getting this in bits and pieces until I'm done eating."

Cassie mumbled her agreement as she stuffed more pizza into her mouth and washed it down with her margarita.

"I was working at a bar called Heaven. It was part of a bar restaurant combination called Heaven and Earth. Obviously the restaurant was Earth. Their specialty was prime rib.

"Like most bars, Heaven had a specific clientele; the state senators and representatives.

"It was located in a downtown high-rise... well, high for Salem."

Cassie finished chewing and swallowed. "Is the bar still there?"

I shook my head. "No, they closed down in 1982."

She took a sip from her margarita. "Would I know where it was at?"

I smiled then chuckled. "Oh, yeah."

Cassie faced me and narrowed her eyes. "What?"

"Listen to my description carefully. The parquet dance floor butted up against the outside floor to ceiling glass windows. There were tables at both ends of the dance floor. Two of the three walls were glass, the third being the only cloth-covered solid wall. The bar, which looked out over the dance floor and the windows, made up the fourth wall of the lounge area. In the center of the dance floor suspended from the ceiling was a mirrored disco ball."

Cassie frowned disgustedly. Then slowly, ever so slowly, her features began to flicker with recognition. Her eyes grew large and widened, looking directly at me.

"You... can't... mean..."

I let a smirk touch the corners of my lips.

"Donald's offices. His entire office complex used to be one of the hottest nightclubs in town."

A furrow creased her forehead.

"But why would that cause you to have such a weird reaction?"

I looked at her concerned eyes.

"Are you sure you want to go into this?"

She leaned over and put her paper plate on the coffee table. After another sip of her margarita, she settled into the couch.

"Where are we going?"

I looked her square in the eyes. "I hope we're still friends after you hear what I have to tell you."

She blew out an exasperated breath.

"Quit stalling."

"Alright, here goes."

Chapter Six

"As I said, I started working at Heaven in 1979. It was the place to be. There were nights it was so busy they kept the lobby on the ground floor full with people waiting to be allowed inside. I was young, thin, pretty and smart enough to use it to my advantage.

"Around the middle of July, I started noticing this muscular, tanned god coming in on Wednesday nights. The bar had something going almost every night of the week and Wednesdays were 'Boys Night Out.' Management had dropped the price of drinks by a dollar and knew if the guys wandered in, the girls would follow.

"Gregg started sitting at my end of the bar."

Cassie raised an eyebrow. "Gregg?"

I nodded. "Gregg Halstrom. We started talking casually at first and I learned he was also a bartender. His days off were Tuesday and Wednesday. At the time mine were Monday and Tuesday.

"He was gorgeous; no doubt about it, but underneath the good looks was education and kindness."

Cassie watched as I drifted away.

~ * ~

"Hey beautiful."

I turned sideways to the counter and held up a finger. Swiping the credit card through the machine, I entered the bill amount. I finished totaling everything on the charge slip and grabbed a pen. Sliding charge slip

22

and pen under the Senator's hand, I waited until he signed. I detached his copy and glanced at the bottom line. A smile crossed my face.

Senator Anderson loved his per diem account. We *all* benefited from his per diem account. I took the twenty dollar bill from the register and turned to blow a kiss the Senator's direction.

"Hey, beautiful. How about a Gregg driver?"

Even over the thumping of the speakers, I knew that voice.

"One Gregg driver coming up."

A Gregg driver--our inside shared secret. Gregg had alcohol issues. A father who beat him senseless every other weekend to '*man you up*', and a mother who brought home new *friends* on the weekends Gregg's dad was out of town had quickly cured him about the coolness of getting drunk.

It had taken a couple months of trust building to get past the glib, smarmy answers he usually gave and get to the truth. He trusted I would never tell a soul, and I wasn't about to blow that trust.

I pulled out a chimney glass, filled it with ice cubes and proceeded to pull a blue-labeled Vodka brand bottle from under the well. Seen only to me was a black X on the label indicating the alcohol free water inside. Flourishing the bottle, I poured a shot and a half of the clear liquid into the glass. I finished by adding orange juice, and popping in a long straw.

Placing the completed drink before him, I waited for him to take a sip and give me the thumbs up.

He took a sip and smiled as he flashed his upturned thumb my direction. "Perfect again, beautiful."

"Thanks."

"Say when are we…"

About the time he started to ask me a question, some blonde bombshell in a very tight lycra skirt up to her… well, you get the idea, draped herself all over Gregg's shoulders.

"Hello, handsome."

"Hello, Misty."

Gregg's monotone response didn't phase her one bit.

She oozed around the barstool and wedged herself between his legs.

"When are we going to dinner?" She leaned over to give him the benefit of a full shot of her cleavage.

I was busy making drinks for the waitresses beginning to jam up at the station on my end of the bar but was able to hear the conversation. I wasn't listening, really I wasn't.

The blonde leaned in and whispered in Gregg's ear.

I watched as his face crimsoned in the dim lighting.

He placed his hands on her waist and guided her to the side of his barstool.

"How many times do I need to tell you, Misty? I don't date customers."

I watched the glow of lust fan into a raging fire of anger in her eyes.

"Well, you won't find anything better, that's for sure." She turned and stomped back to her table.

I glanced out of the corner of my eye as she poured out her tale to the two girls sitting with her. After much consoling and sending of dirty looks Gregg's direction, the trio picked up their purses and left.

Gregg leaned against the barstool back, pushing an exasperated breath through his lips.

"Man, they are like sharks on a blood trail." He ran long, slender fingers through his dark locks.

"Sorry, luv, but with girls like Misty, kindness will always be mistaken for lust. It's a game the locals play of bartender-notching. She figures if you give in to her obvious charms…"

"Obvious." He rolled his eyes.

I shot a glare his direction. He rewarded me with a grin that featured the dimple in his right cheek.

"As I was saying… once you have partaken of her indescribable delights, you'll fall madly in love with her, give her all her drinks for free then marry her and buy her a big house in South Salem."

Gregg arched an eyebrow.

I filled a couple dozen drink orders. When there was a lull in the din and the disc jockey had decided to slow the pace down, he motioned me over to him.

I pulled a glass out and made another Gregg driver, which I took and placed in front of him.

"On me."

He quirked a lopsided smile my direction.

"I wish."

"I thought you didn't date customers.

"You're not a …"

He stopped at the look I was shooting him.

"What do you call me coming to your bar and listening to music?"

"Well, that's different."

"How, Gregg?"

"Well, you're a bartender."

I smirked. I loved watching him wriggle under the scrutiny.

"It's different because you're a fellow professional."

"Great. Now you're calling me a guy."

"Ah…ah…ah…"

I couldn't keep up the charade and broke out laughing. I could see color flushing his face. He gave up and started laughing along with me. While we giggled, I spied a familiar shuffle and was enveloped by the accompanying sickly sweet cloud of cologne.

I knew this customer dubbed--*the Strange One*--by my coworkers for his unusual obsession, and grabbed a long neck beer for him. I took the bottle to the bar where I opened it in front of him then handed it to him.

The blocky, sandy-haired young man nodded at me.

"Lucy."

"Richard. How are you today?"

"I'm fine, thank you. It's been a productive day. I gathered enough cans to have two beers tonight."

"That's terrific, Richard. Would you excuse me? I see I have some orders to fill."

"That would be fine, Lucy. See you in a while?"

"For certain, Richard."

Moving to my workstation, I noted his usually stringy hair was neatly combed and tucked behind his ears. I wasn't sure what color his eyes were but in the dark of the bar, they appeared to be light. Clean new slacks and a shirt with a bit of style replaced his disheveled clothing.

My observations were cut short by a flurry of drink orders and the throbbing of music punctuated with the spinning lights from the disco floor. The mirrored disco ball flashed in my face and I felt sweat created by the overabundance of bodies and cigarette smoke in the room meandering its way down my chest. An hour and, who knows how many drinks later, I pulled Willow, my coworker and friend, aside.

"I need a break."

She quickly completed a visual survey of the room and its occupants.

"Got it handled."

"Richard…"

"Oh, no. The Strange One is here?"

"Yes. If he starts asking for me…"

I glanced past her and noted he was staring at the dance floor--the opposite of where I was standing.

"… tell him I've gone to the bathroom. That should keep him from flipping out."

Willow looked his direction and shivered.

"It would give me the creeps if he liked me. How do you handle it?"

I looked past her to the solitary figure clutching the brown bottle and tracking dancers with his eyes. *Still distracted--good.*

I moved past her, using her body as a shield. "With kid gloves. Back in twenty."

Bolting to the end of the bar and flipping up the counter, I indicated Gregg should follow me with minimal motion of my forefinger.

He lifted his brows and drink. With a barely perceptible nod, I motioned him to bring the glass along.

We slipped around the corner to a narrow hallway leading to a locked door. Using my passkey, I opened the kitchen passageway of the adjoining restaurant. The night chef raised a knife in acknowledgement as he diced parsley. I fixed a soda and led Gregg to an empty table overlooking the Capitol rotunda.

"How in the world did you convince that crazy guy to take an open beer from you?"

"What do you mean?" Richard was not who I wanted to talk about.

"How did you get him to take an open beer from you?"

"Gregg, you're repeating yourself. Richard's always taken opened beers from me. I'm sure he does it with everyone. Just ask Willow."

Gregg vigorously shook his head. "No. I've worked behind the bar in two or three clubs around town and I've never seen the Strange One accept an opened container.

"Most of us have learned to open the cooler, let him watch us pick a bottle, get his approval on the choice then hand him the opener so he can open his own. He won't drink otherwise."

I realized as I was looking at him my jaw was hanging open.

"You're joking, right?"

"No. He thinks somebody's trying to poison him."

"He's never had a problem with me opening his beer bottle."

"And he talks to you."

"Yeah, so?"

"Most of the rest of us get grunts or head nods. Must be he likes you."

Gregg let a smirk slide across his lips.

"Now I know you're exaggerating. I just treat Richard like a human being and he appreciates it, that's all. Anyway, I didn't take a break to talk about him. I took a break so we could talk… quietly."

I gazed into those beautiful eyes ringed in black lashes.

Gregg slid his hand across the table and pulled mine into his clutch.

"Listen, Lucy. We've been tap dancing around the obvious. Will you have dinner with me? We're both off tomorrow. I could pick you up around noon and we could drive to the coast. That way, no one would see us."

I had to smile. In a single sentence, he had covered all my objections

"Okay. Have you something to write with so I can jot down my address? Pen, pencil, blood?"

He retrieved a pen and small tablet from inside his jacket pocket, which he slid across the tabletop to me.

I wrote my address and phone number in the notebook.

"Absolutely, positively do *not* give this to anyone. I jealously guard my privacy. I don't want every *gonna-make-you-a-star* creep calling me."

He pulled the tablet to him and snapped the pen closed.

"Not a chance. I've waited three months to get this number. I have no intentions of sharing it with anyone." He patted his pocket. "I'll see you at eleven."

He winked and smirked into his drink.

Glancing at my watch, I realized I was reaching the end of my break.

"As much as I'd love to spend the next four hours right here… I have to go back--alone--and try to avoid Richard."

Gregg rose from the table. "How about I visit the boys' room? That should give you enough time…"

The chef bustled up to the table, bearing a silver platter inside a wooden holder; sizzling slices of tantalizing beef wafting a cloud of peppered deliciousness. "Lucy, I know you're on break but I've tried several times to get the attention of somebody out there to pick up these steak fingers. Would you take them back to the bar? Thanks."

I grabbed the platter with potholders and moved toward the bar. Gregg followed me as far as the hallway where he split and headed to the men's room.

When I entered the cacophony of lights and sound, I stopped. A quick straightening of my shoulders and pasting of a smile on my face put me back in the working mode. Carrying the platter to the waitress station, I caught Willow's attention with a lift of my eyebrow.

She maneuvered a quick eye roll and mouthed, *Don Knight's,* over the noise.

I sucked in a deep breath. *Great, Mr. Hands.* Notorious for his ability to have his hands in more places than a teenage octopus, Don Knight was not a popular customer despite his overly large tipping habit.

I ferried the platter to Don's table where he sat next to a blonde sporting large hair, large blue eyes, large platform heels and… other large attributes.

"Lucy, babe…"

I cringed at the over familiar use of my name.

"Don, steak fingers with fries and barbeque sauce. That'll be $7.95."

I placed the platter on the table and stood, hands on hips.

"Babe…" Don grinned and slid his hand toward my butt. "Sit and talk. Bobbi here is great to look at but not much on conversation. Right, doll?"

The blonde shrugged her shoulders, her attention never leaving the dance floor.

I grabbed the hand residing on my posterior and placed it on the table.

"Don, I'm working. Just pay me so I can get to my other customers."

His hand inched toward me. I put my fingers on Don's moving appendage effectively stopping the motion. I leaned over, watching his gaze drop from my own and come to rest on my exposed cleavage. Leaning close to him, I put my body weight on the hand beneath mine.

The lascivious expression melted into a painful grimace.

"If…" I dropped the volume of my voice causing him to lean closer, the movement created excruciating pressure on his trapped digits. The grimace pulled his mouth down at the edges creeping to his eyes.

"… if you create a scene, I'll guarantee you will be 86'd from this establishment for life. Are we clear?"

Nodding his head furiously, Don jerked his hand from the tabletop the moment I straightened and released it.

Reaching into the pocket of a pair of ironed jeans that sported a razor sharp crease, he extracted a faux alligator wallet. Maneuvering with his undamaged extremity, he fumbled to pull out a twenty dollar bill which he handed to me.

"Keep the change."

I snatched the bill from his hand. With my back to Don, I flashed Willow a huge smile.

Surveying the patrons seated at the bar, I noted Gregg was not among them.

Willow waved an arm grabbing my attention. At the end of her shapely limb, clutched in her slender fingers, was a piece of paper.

I worked my way behind the bar and snatched the folded note from her fingertips.

"Lucy,
Gonna call it a night. Big plans for tomorrow. See you at eleven. I'll bring breakfast."

G."

Goose bumps rose on my arms and the hair on the back of my neck stood on end. Someone was watching me. Looking up, I found Willow, left eyebrow quirked, peering my direction.

"Well?" she mouthed over the roar of music and dancers.

The DJ was pumping up the crowd by playing back-to-back *Earth, Wind and Fire* tunes. The din was deafening.

I tilted my head and let a smile play over my lips. *Let her stew.* I turned to step from behind the bar and pick up empty glasses around the room.

There he stood, immobile and staring directly at me.

I jumped.

"Richard, you, uh, gave me a start. Are you okay? Need anything?"

"Where were you?" He stared unblinking into my eyes.

"Beg pardon?"

"Where… were… you?" His mouth was an angry slash across his face. I watched a muscle in his jaw line flex and relax alternately.

Pulling myself to my full 5'3", if you count heels 5'6", I glared at him.

"It's really none of your business."

Violent emotions crossed his face, causing me to rethink my answer. He settled on disgust.

"I was worried. You know how dangerous this building can be."

His veiled reference to several recently reported rapes in the building's stairwells gave me pause. I hadn't considered the idea. Softening my ire, I answered him.

"I was in the restroom."

He huffed disbelief and walked away from the bar.

I whipped around to stare at Willow.

The DJ had opted to cool the fury of the dancers with a slow song. I wasn't sure if the music was cooling them down or heating up their hormones.

"Willow!"

The sharpness of my tone stopped her movement behind the bar and she looked up at me.

"What!?"

"How long was…" I turned and surveyed the area around me then faced her "…the Strange One hovering?"

She shrugged away impatience. "Long enough to see you leave with Gregg."

"Damn! I don't need him trying to save me."

I charged out to the floor and gathered all the empty bottles and glasses I could carry on my tray. I'd become so caught up in the order and serve routine, I stopped in my tracks when I heard the DJ announce last call.

Fifteen minutes of pandemonium followed with patrons determined to get one last drink.

Once the lights were turned up, there was the inevitable scurrying for hook-ups; no one wanted to go home alone. I plowed through the drunk and nearly drunk bodies trying to get a head start on clean up. If Willow and I worked together, we could be walking out the door around three a.m. The DJ waved as she left on the arm of her third conquest that week. They were a striking pair, both over six feet tall, dark and tanned.

We chased the last customer from the bar and locked the doors to count the money in the register and our tips.

"So…"

When Willow started a sentence with *so,* I knew I was in trouble.

"So, what?" I ran a calculator tape of my drink tickets.

"Oh, don't be coy. It doesn't suit you. What's the story with Gregg?"

I held up a finger as I finished totaling up my food tickets.

"What was your question? I was busy *working.*"

Willow rolled her eyes and flipped her hair over one shoulder.

"Lucy, anyone who has eyes can see the flames roar when the two of you are together. Are you going to start dating or what?"

I finished my paperwork by putting my money and receipts together then dropping the bundle in the bank bag, which I handed to Willow.

"Here. I'm done. Could I get a daiquiri-on-the-rocks for my shift drink?"

"No."

"What?" I looked up from organizing my tips to find her shaking her head.

"Not until you give me the story on you and Gregg."

The glare emanating from her eyes and crossed arms warned me I needed to give her details or she would hold me down and apply fire to the soles of my feet.

I was too tired to argue.

"Okay, okay. We have our first date tomorrow…"

Her eyes lit up. "That's so cool."

I sent her a smoldering look.

"If anyone breathes a word of this, I'll hunt them down and string them up by their thumbs. Are we clear?"

"Crystal."

"Good. Let's go home."

I gathered my purse and slipped on my jacket as I headed to the time clock. Punching my time card, I strolled down the hallway to the elevator lobby. Willow came puffing up as the doors opened.

We caught up on the evening's activities and went opposite directions at the front door.

I had my keys in hand as I marched to the space where my car was parked.

The spots reserved for employees weren't completely enclosed and the echo of my footsteps gave me goose skin.

There had been a recent rash of rapes and attempted rapes in and around the building. I was highly aware of the rumors. I bent down and squinted my eyes to make sure my key slid into the lock smoothly. The lights from the parking lot were supposed to provide a sense of security, but, as usual, only one third of them were lit and working. *So much for security.* I turned my key and grabbed the door handle when I heard it--a footstep.

Straightening up, I looked around. Mine was the only car in the garage.

Hearing things.

I grabbed the handle and pulled it open. I bent to crawl in the driver's side. That's when things went sideways.

I sucked in a deep breath and let out a blood-curdling scream.

Chapter Seven

The hand on my shoulder dropped as I wriggled free and dived into my car, slamming the door behind me. My heart thudded against my chest and I could taste the cigarette smoke clinging to my clothing. Jamming the key into the ignition, the engine roared to life as I tried to ignore the knocking on my window.

The sooner I'm out of here, the happier I'll be. Sweat trickled down the back of my shirt.

I shoved in the clutch and, turning to back out of the spot, discovered myself face-to-face with Richard.

Stuttered breaths escaped my mouth as I stomped on the brake and rested my head on the steering wheel to slow my staccato heartbeat. Pulling air deeply into my lungs, the panic oozed from my feet through the floorboards. I pulled myself to a sitting position and inched my window down just enough to speak.

"What do you need, Richard?"

He turned lifeless eyes my direction. "I was watching to make sure you made it to your car safely."

With a deftness I didn't feel, I moved the gearshift back into reverse and allowed my foot to ease the clutch back.

"Thank you, Richard. You scared the hell out of me. I'm going to go home now. I'm *very* tired."

He stepped away from the side of the car and watched as I backed out and left the parking garage.

I glanced into my rearview mirror. He stood with his feet shoulder width apart, hands dangling at his sides, the garage lights framing his wild hair. The expression on his face sent shivers down my spine as his cold eyes tracked my departure.

Checking myself to keep from speeding, I cranked up the volume of the radio allowing the throbbing beat of the disco song to drown my qualms. My vehicle slid into the parking space of the apartment complex and I peeled my fingers from the steering wheel. Turning off my lights, I sat in the darkness, my eyes moving to my rearview and side mirrors. Just thinking Richard had followed me set my heart racing and blood pressure to soaring. I could smell my own fear… or was it just the stale smell of old beer and cigarettes?

In either case, I needed to be in a safe, comfortable place. Once out of the car, which I locked and checked twice, I bounded up the steps to my third floor apartment. There was no way he could ambush me here.

I hurried inside locking the deadbolt and securing the chain. Keys and purse landed on the kitchen counter as I peeled my work clothing off and headed for the shower. Hot water peppering my muscles forced me to relax. The vision of Richard's cold eyes following me sent a shiver through me despite the steam filled room.

"A couple aspirins and a shot of tequila should knock me out." The sound of my voice echoed hollowly in the porcelain-lined space. I toweled dry, rubbing my skin until it glowed pink and slipped beneath cool, clean sheets allowing the exhaustion of the night to overtake me. My last coherent thought was of Gregg's sparkling eyes.

~ * ~

Outside the apartment door, the silhouetted figure slipped the single red rose between the doorframe and doorknob. An envelope was propped against the door.

As quietly as the figure had ascended the stairs, it descended and disappeared into the night.

~ * ~

I groaned as the beeping of the alarm tore me from my dreamworld.

"All right, all right."

I reached over and smacked the offending noisemaker. My eyes began to drift close when a fleeting thought penetrated the haze.

"Gregg!"

He was scheduled to be here in forty-five minutes. I couldn't take any chances he'd arrive early and catch me without make up. I zipped through my morning routine and was sipping coffee when a knock on the door, at the appointed time, interrupted my morning solace.

I felt my heart flutter and my stomach tap dance.

"Just a minute!"

A quick mirror check proved everything was where I had planned it to be. I went to open the door.

There he stood--in his dry cleaned jeans, polo shirt snuggly showing off his broad chest, and holding a single rose and envelope.

Smiling, I opened the door for him to enter.

"How sweet, Gregg."

I took the rose and he handed me the envelope.

"I'd like to take credit for this, but I can't. It was here when I arrived."

I whirled around to face him.

"What?"

"Yeah. The rose was propped against the knob and the envelope was leaning on the door."

For a moment, his words made no sense. I stood clutching the rose.

"Why don't you open the envelope?" he closed the door behind him.

My hand trembled as I pulled out the flap and retrieved the folded paper inside.

"Watching your back. Richard."

I dropped the note, the rose slicing my finger as it fell. A drop of blood hit the carpet.

"Damn it!"

Gregg quirked an eyebrow and concern washed over his face.

"Lucy? What's the matter?"

I headed to the kitchen and grabbed a towel, which I threw to him.

"Could you get that blood off the carpet, please?" I dampened another kitchen towel with cold water after washing away the blood on my finger and moved to the entry to ensure the blood would not stain the rug.

"Sorry, Gregg."

"Lucy, what's happening?"

He reached down and picked up the note. I watched his eyes scan over the words.

"Richard? Who's Richard?" A dangerous undertone crept into his question.

Rising from my crouched position, I grabbed the rose and snatched the note from his hands crumpling the paper. I held up the balled wad.

"The Strange One."

The expression of distrust slipped from his face.

Stomping to the kitchen, I tossed the flower and crumpled note in the trashcan.

I was headed to the bathroom, head down and frowning when I bumped into a muscular roadblock.

A finger tucked beneath my chin and lifted it up. My eyes looked into a set of worried blue orbs.

"Lucy?"

The deep, smooth voice quieted the butterflies dive-bombing my stomach.

Gregg slipped an arm around my waist and pulled me to him. The heat of his body penetrated my jeans and sweater.

My heart thudded against my ribs. Lightheadedness threatened to carry me away.

Dropping his finger and hand to pull me closer, he lowered his head and placed his soft lips against mine.

I sagged against his warm form and allowed the secure sensation I was feeling to wrap around me.

His tongue touched the crease of my lips hesitantly. I welcomed his quest with enthusiasm. My arms slid around his neck and I molded my body to his. My eyes shuttered closed.

I felt a hand creep down to cup my bottom. A fire I could never have imagined was raging in my soul. I didn't want this moment to end. It became increasingly evident Gregg was feeling a fire of his own.

He broke the kiss and leaned back.

"Lucy, I don't want us to start out like this."

"I don't mind."

"I do."

I had to take a step back. *A man saying no to sex?* My heart flip-flopped. If I thought I liked him previously, I was afraid I might be falling in love now. A smile began to form on my lips.

"Thank you."

Gregg winked.

"I'm not saying no forever… just not today."

I smirked. "Good."

His mirthful expression faded.

"What's this thing with Richard?"

"Let's talk about it on our way out. I feel as though there are watchful eyes everywhere."

I gathered up my purse and a jacket with gloves and scarf tucked in the pockets. One never knew what the weather would be at the coast. It could be ninety degrees in Salem, but by the time you arrived at the coast, the breeze from the ocean would cool the temperature to sixty; add clouds and sea spray and the difference was phenomenal.

We left the apartment, me locking and double-checking every window and door. Within thirty minutes, Salem and Richard, the Strange One, were memories.

The drive to the coast was always cathartic for me. Rolling knolls gave way to evergreen covered mountains. In checkered patches over the peaks, logging operations had clear-cut down to the roadway leaving gaping holes in the blanket of greenery.

The saving grace of the ride was the H.B. Van Duzer corridor. A twelve-mile stretch of protected State Park, the Van Duzer would soothe the soul of the devil himself.

Gregg and I made small talk, commenting on mutual bar patrons and latest gossip rounding the nightclub scene. We talked about schedules and going-back-to-college plans. We talked about any and everything but the obvious.

I knew if I didn't address the elephant sitting in the car with us, the purpose of the day would be lost.

"Last night as I was walking to my car, I had the distinct feeling of being watched."

Gregg glanced sideways at me.

I pulled in a deep breath and continued.

"I looked around and couldn't see anyone. When I started to open the car door, I heard footsteps. Whipping around still didn't reveal anyone so I hustled into the car and closed the door. As I started to pull out of the parking spot, there was a tapping on my window.

"I nearly had a heart attack. Richard was standing next to my car."

Gregg snapped his head around to stare at me. We'd just passed the road sign noting the rest stop located half a mile ahead. With the ease of a professional, he guided the car to the turn lane and exited. Parking under the trees, he turned to face me.

"Lucy?" There was a dangerous edge to his tone.

"What?"

"Why didn't you call me?"

I squirmed under his scrutiny. The air in the car felt heavy and I knew no matter what I said… would be wrong.

"Gregg…"

"Well?"

I cleared my throat and wiggled in the seat.

"… it was 3:30 in the morning and I had the situation handled."

"Apparently not. Did you know he followed you home?"

"No, but…"

"Then the situation may have been put on hold, but you can guarantee it's not finished."

I blew out a deep breath and gazed out the side window. I had wanted this day to be relaxing, quiet and provide the start of a good, possibly long, relationship.

The warmth of his hand on mine stopped the tears pooling in my eyes.

"I'm not angry, just scared. Richard is not right in the head. One of the gals I work with has seen him around town for a couple years, and she commented no one seems to have reached him like you.

"He may get really possessive and who knows where that will lead. Lucy… I really care for you."

Something in his voice made me turn and let his gaze capture me.

The beautiful blue eyes were clouded with concern. Small lines across his forehead added to the seriousness of his statement. His brows furrowed together.

"I've just found you. I can't afford to have anything happen to you now."

My heart lurched. Here was a guy admitting he cared for me. All my survival instincts went on hold. Now what?

I relaxed and allowed a nervous smile to touch my lips.

"If you want me to call you, should this happen again, I will. But by the time I get home and call, it'll be over." I shrugged my shoulders.

Gregg's slow smile warmed the space in the car's interior. The worry lines disappeared and his eyes lit up.

"Let's go to Moe's for lunch."

I leaned back in the plush bucket seat.

"Sounds great."

Gregg squeezed my hand and winked.

"This is going to be a great day. I promise."

That's what I wanted to hear.

Chapter Eight

The door slammed, the sound echoing against the bare walls. A slumped figure shuffled in the room and plunked down a green garbage bag, aluminum cans clinking noisily. Each lock slid satisfactorily into the matching bolt receptacle. He trundled to the kitchen area and threw the bag in a corner populated by similar green holders.

Leaning over the sink, taking great care not to touch the counter, he used his index fingertip and thumb to turn on the hot water faucet. He proceeded to stick his hands under the scalding liquid, holding them in position until he saw the dark spots before his eyes that usually signaled he was about to pass out. With a forefinger, he stopped the flow of the steaming liquid and stood letting the liquid drip off his hands into the sink.

"Must be more careful next time. Can't... touch... anything. Flower..."

He shuddered.

"...DDT. Door has millions of germs."

His eyes darted wildly about the room as his feet began moving.

The extensions at the end of his arms were swollen an angry red. Skin had begun to blister and peel, and he knew if he bumped them they would bleed. But he needed to go--really bad.

Bleeding was acceptable. It would flush away the poison. Wetting himself was not. It would result in punishment. He flinched at the memories of childhood so vivid he could feel the sting of the belt leather and unconsciously gritted his teeth against the sharp pain of the buckle hitting his raw, wet skin.

He walked stiff legged to the small bathroom. After relieving himself, he examined his throbbing hands. They hadn't bled. He must be toughening up.

Richard would have to be tough if he was to protect Lucy from the danger.

He growled through a grimace.

"Why don't they learn? If she surrounds herself with evil, I'll be forced to protect her from those forces.

"They only seek the pure ones."

He gingerly pulled the shirt over his head, tossing it in the trashcan when he'd freed himself from the material. His jeans followed.

"Poisoned, deadly, bad."

Turning every light in the small studio apartment on, he curled up on his plastic wrap covered couch. He drew his knees to his chest, shivering in the cold room.

"Need to turn on the heat."

"NO! Germs, poison."

He lay shivering until his eyes closed and he floated to the land free of worry.

A new face invaded his sleep time. That bartender from Lucky's, Gregg. This was one he needed to keep an eye on.

Richard could sense the danger. In his dream world, he warned the Lady Lucy and she came to his side after he ran his blade through the evil Gregg.

He needed to be cautious and watch the man. His Lady Love was in danger.

Chapter Nine

Oregon Coast--Lincoln City

We silently watched the waves crash over the rocks at the bay's opening. Gulls swooped crazily in the sky and a nearby tourist pointed out a sea otter playing in the current.

Moe's famous clam chowder essence permeated the restaurant, bringing hunger pains to the stomach and alerting the taste buds.

I dug my spoon into the thick, creamy concoction and wrapped my lips around the taste of heaven on earth.

"Hmmmm." Closing my eyes, I let the flavors dance across my tongue and waft through my olfactory sensors. I could pick out the individual sensations: plump clams, real butter, rich cream, tangy pepper and sharp scallions. The list was endless. I opened my eyes to find Gregg smiling at me.

"Good?"

"Divine. What?"

He chuckled, a warm, bubbly sound welling up from deep in his chest.

"I've never seen anyone make eating clam chowder so... sexy."

I felt the heat flare to my cheeks.

"Good food is supposed to be enjoyed."

"And you enjoy it so... lustily."

"I swear you're trying to embarrass me."

He leaned toward me, his elbows on the table.

"No. Your honest actions surprise me. Can't say I've run into a woman who actually eats when she's hungry."

I sniffed.

"They also don't belch, pass gas, sweat, use the bathroom or blow their noses. It's amazing our society has survived all these centuries."

I jumped when he burst into laughter.

"That's what I mean." The lights in his eyes danced. "You have no problem admitting you're human."

"If I want this situation to progress beyond hand holding, I'd better damn well admit I'm human."

I finished the chowder and put the spoon on the table.

"I think I might still be hungry but I'll wait. Might make you buy me pie a la mode at Chalet."

Gregg slid a hand across the top of the picnic-style table, slipping it beneath mine. I noted the mischievous twinkle had been replaced by an intense stare meant to penetrate my defenses. I sensed a yearning as deep as my own.

"I know you think I might be putting you off about the physical side of our relationship, but Lucy…"

He bundled my hand in his and placed a gentle kiss on the top.

"… this…" he circled his hand to encompass the both of us. "… you, to be specific, are too important to me to throw away on a momentary lapse of judgment and physical gratification."

I found myself at a loss for words. I'd never run into any man who would turn down a no-strings-attached, roll-in-the-hay.

A smile slowly spread across his handsome face. My heart thudded against my ribs. This man was worming his way into my soul with alarming ease. I threw out a suggestion.

"Why don't we get out of here?"

He winked at me. "Making you uncomfortable?"

Beneath the dark lashes ringing his eyes, the cobalt blue orbs twinkled deviously.

"No, my butt's going numb."

Gregg laughed. "Oh, sure." He swooped up the meal ticket as I reached for it.

I threw him a thunderous frown. "Let me get lunch."

He shook his head, his lopsided grin spreading. "No way. I invited you. This is my treat. I need to make a stop first, then we'll go."

I watched him stroll to the restroom, the firm muscles of his bottom undulating enticingly beneath his jeans with each step.

A sigh escaped my lips. His long, easy strides brought back aching memories of the man I'd left behind in California; a total abandonment of common sense on my part. I was lost in the musing when he returned.

"Wow! You look a million miles away."

I'd been reliving the last painful day with my ex, startled when Gregg broke my reverie. Color rushed to my face.

"Just watching the gulls playing tag."

Gregg's eyes swept over my reddened face. He held out a hand.

"If you say so, Lucy. What say we take a walk on the beach?"

I accepted his hand and allowed myself to be lifted from the bench.

"Sounds good. Probably should work off this chowder before it settles permanently on my hips."

Gregg rolled his eyes. "I like your hips."

I had the good sense to accept his compliment graciously. "Thank you."

We took our coats from the hooks near the door and bundled up. The fog wall off the beach was slowly masking the weak sunshine.

He moved his arm to my shoulders and snugged me to his body. I could feel his heat through our clothing... or was it just my imagination?

We strolled out the walkway toward the open ocean. The closer to the beach we ventured, the more the wind picked up. My hair whipped around my face and I shivered involuntarily. Gregg enveloped me in his arms.

"I think it's time to go back and get warm."

My teeth started to chatter. "I'd argue with you but I'm too cold."

We hustled to the car, sitting for about ten minutes as the heater worked magic on our frozen extremities.

"Now what?" Gregg wiggled his eyebrows at me.

I giggled at his silliness. He was more relaxed than the image he projected in Salem. I liked the Salem Gregg, but I felt myself beginning to fall hard for this real, uninhibited Gregg.

"Let's work our way back to home; maybe walk along the tourist shops on Lincoln City's main drag, stopping for salt water taffy before we go home. Can't make a trip to the Coast and not get taffy."

"Your wish is my command. To the tourist traps and beyond."

I laughed, amazed at how relaxed I felt. Since I'd moved from California and away from my ex, I'd been walking a fine line between a deep blue funk and the sensation of giddy freedom.

It had been a couple years since my arrival in Oregon and my choices in male companions had been--questionable at best.

Gregg stood head and shoulders above all of them. What had I done right?

Not wanting to think too hard, I looked past Gregg to the changing scenery. The Oregon Coast wasn't the same in any two places; it undulated around land points offering pristine sandy stretches great for walking or presented rocky outcroppings where waves crashed with wild intensity.

In some spots, the homes were built right up to the beaches, while half an acre away woods grew to the edges of the cliffs. The sky served to teach disbelievers there *is* more than one shade of gray.

Finding a parking spot on the street in front of the stores, we stopped.

Gregg turned to me. "Don't get out."

It was my turn to raise my eyebrows. "Beg pardon?"

"*Please* don't get out."

He walked around the back of the car then opened my door, offering me his hand.

"Shall we?"

The last time I'd had a man open my door was… hell, I couldn't remember. I grinned as he helped lift me from the bucket seat.

"Worth the wait."

He bent down and locked the car. Straightening, he winked. "Of course."

I rolled my eyes. "Good heavens."

We broke up laughing and headed for the first curio store on the block. The rest of the afternoon, we wandered aimlessly through the shops, commenting about the stuff people bought when on vacation. I purchased salt-water taffy and Gregg disappeared for about fifteen minutes. When he sauntered back to the car, he held something behind his back as he opened my door. All my efforts to try and sneak a peek were met with resistance. I gave up.

Winding down the road on the way out of town, I let a big sigh escape.

"Whoa… what's that all about?" Gregg glanced at me, a worry line marring his forehead.

"Oh, nothing. It's been such a perfect day; I really hate having to go back to Salem. Everything will go back to the way it was." An overwhelming urge to cry pushed at me. My throat tightened and I fought tears.

We rode in silence to the rest stop. I flung open the door the moment the vehicle stopped and bolted to the bathroom. As it was the middle of the week, the number of people visiting the facilities was minimal.

I skirted into an open stall and locked the door behind me. I couldn't stop the flood of tears. Gregg's acts of tenderness all day brought feelings to the forefront I'd been trying to ignore for a couple years.

Did I allow myself to care again? Last time I'd given in to my emotions, I'd been hurt, deeply hurt. Was I rebounding? The wall I'd erected was pretty thick and tall enough most guys didn't try to vault it. But I already knew Gregg wasn't *most guys*.

I pulled in a deep breath and wet a paper towel with the coldest water I could get from the faucet. I dabbed at the puffy bags I knew had formed beneath my red-rimmed eyes. I fluffed my hair and put on some lip-gloss I always carried in my pocket. Squaring my shoulders, I headed to the car half wondering if he'd still be there.

He was leaning his back against the vehicle, eyes closed, an expression of pure joy on his face. Red tones highlighted by the sun glowed in his hair. His strong profile stopped me in my tracks.

Damn, he's good-looking.

I cleared my throat and he opened his eyes.

"Hey, Lucy. Been there long?"

His blue eyes sparkled.

"Naw," I lied. "Just got here. Didn't realize I needed this stop until you pulled into the parking lot. Thanks."

He chuckled, the warm sound caressing my ears.

"It's a trick I learned when I started coming to the coast. You don't realize how much you need this stop until you *don't* make it. I'm not one hundred percent ready to go back. Why don't we sit at the picnic table for a bit?"

A lopsided smile from me encouraged him to lead me by the hand to the brook that flowed at the base of the rising mountains. Old trees provided a canopy of shade. Sitting on one side of the bench, we allowed the sound of running water to make the conversation.

He turned to face me, reaching into his pocket and retrieving something he held in the palm of his hand.

"This had been one of the best days I've hand in longer than I can remember. Lucy, please say we can continue to see each other?"

The intensity of his gaze set my pulse to racing. I measured my words carefully.

"I don't see why we can't. We'll just have to be careful. You know how active the rumor mill is in town."

I noted a twinge of sadness around his eyes.

"I've blown it, haven't I? All this *won't date a customer* stuff is chasing you away, isn't it?"

"No. I'm just careful with my heart… maybe too careful."

Gregg placed a squat square box on the table.

"Open it, please, Lucy."

I pulled the box toward me and removed the lid.

"Gregg, you shouldn't have! It's much too expensive!"

My eyes took in the wide turquoise and agate encrusted silver band. I'd admired the fine workmanship in the store back in Lincoln City.

"You like it?" Earnest eyes raked my face.

"I love it. But…"

"But nothing. I've had a terrific day and want to savor this time with you. When I see you wear this bracelet, which I know you love, I'll smile and remember our escape to the coast.

"Please don't tell me to take it back."

I gazed at a pair of enormous, pleading eyes. I couldn't help myself. I let the smile I'd been biting back escape.

"I'll never be able to tell you no."

Gregg's expression melted to mischievousness.

"I was hoping you'd say that. Now, I have you in my evil clutches!"

He wiggled his eyebrows at me and our laughter reverberated through the woods.

Chapter Ten

Salem

Luminescence from the streetlight filtered through dirt streaked windows, the humming of the refrigerator breaking the cloaking silence of the dingy apartment.

Spartan furniture, arms shiny from years of assorted hands gripping the thinly veneered wood and threadbare material on the sagging cushions, stood as lonely sentinels in the room. The occupant slid his flashlight from beneath the battered couch. Crawling on gloved hands and brown bag-covered knees to the windowsill; he peered warily at the rosy fingers of dawn creeping over the rooftops of the city.

Soon he would be forced to lower the heavy, lined velvet curtains to keep out prying eyes… and the germs. The daylight encouraged them to come out from their hiding places. No one else could see them, but Richard had caught them overrunning his clothing. He'd had to burn his clothes, and the house, because his parents just didn't understand how dangerous the germs could be.

It was sad they'd been burned, too, but… he'd warned and they hadn't listened. The germs had infected their bodies and minds. After all, he'd had to protect himself.

Yeah, he knew most people thought he was crazy but it was okay. They'd all die from the poison the germs made. Then who'd be crazy?

Richard reached up with the gloved finger of his left hand and loosened the drapery tieback, whooshing out the air he'd been holding in his lungs. He crawled to the far side of the window and performed the same act on the opposite side. Plunging the room into darkness, he stood and flicked on the flashlight. A narrow band of ambient radiance cut through the black. Guiding himself to the small refrigerator in the kitchenette, he reached into the thickly iced freezer unit, pulled out a glass with his left hand, gently peeling his gloved fingers from the frozen glassware. Placing the vessel on the counter top completely wrapped in plastic, he opened the special aluminum lined drawer, removing a baggie containing a white cotton cloth. Using his right, gloved hand, he flicked the folded cloth open and placed it over the mouth of the glassware. He moved to the refrigerator and pulled out a bottle of water. Being careful not to disturb the cloth covering the glass, Richard held it while straining water from the container through his germ killer.

He settled into a single chair facing the faux fifties chrome table as he let the water settle in the tumbler. He glanced into the living area of his apartment and felt the bile rise in his throat. Daylight was filching into the room around the edges of the curtains. Richard bit his lip.

"I mustn't react. I need to breath... slowly. If they sense my fear, they'll overpower my mind. I--don't--want--to--go--back."

The quietly spoken thought ended in a barely audible whisper.

He took a small sip of the fluid in the water glass through the white cotton cloth. The acrid taste in his mouth puckered his lips and made his eyes water but he considered it a small sacrifice to keep away the germs.

If only it was as easy to protect *her*. Richard allowed a smile to flicker across his lips. She was perfect--well, almost. If he could just keep her from the likes of the dark haired bartender. He couldn't understand why she acted so dumb around that guy. Couldn't she see he was just using her?

Richard began to hum a song his folks repeatedly played on the record player when he was a kid that reminded him of her. It was a Beatles song. His parents really liked the Beatles and played their music all the time.

He'd learned the words to all the songs on all the albums and could still remember them.

But it didn't seem to help him with her. How could he keep her from drifting away?

He thought as he sipped his water slowly. *Of course!* He sat back in his chair, pleased he'd found such a simple solution. He stood then dumped the water down the drain. It was time to sleep. Yawning, he lay on his daybed, dropping his brownbag covered feet to the floor. The windows and doors were safely covered and he'd solved his biggest problem. The best way to keep her safe was diamonds. He drifted to sleep a smile perched on his face and her song circling his brain.

Lucy in the sky with diamonds.

Chapter Eleven

2011

I looked unseeing at the cluttered coffee table, empty pizza boxes and crumpled napkins littering the top. I couldn't remember the last time I'd talked about... hell, I still couldn't even say it in my mind.

Cassie looked at me bleary-eyed. "Then what happened?"

"Girlfriend, I'm exhausted and, by the looks of it, you are too. How about we pick this up later?" A quick glance at the clock revealed just how late, make that early, it was--3 a.m.

The sensation of cold wetness on my upper arm sliced through my memory fog. I turned to find myself staring into the darkest, brownest pair of eyes.

"You're right baby. It's time for you to go out."

Cassie yawned. "Yeah, I could do with some shuteye. Don't think you're off the hook, missy. You promised to tell me why you're acting so weird and I expect the story, the whole story, before the end of the weekend."

Unfolding her legs and standing, she pulled the fluffy robe tight.

"You've been here enough you know where everything is. You're on your own. See you later this morning, if I feel like it, or this afternoon."

Her fuzzy slippers shooshed against the hardwood floor as she stumbled to her bedroom.

I took Tessa, her tail wagging, to the door off the kitchen where we went out to the half acre of manicured lawn. As she paced back and forth searching for the perfect spot to do her business, I stretched my hands over my head, lifting my face to the sky, feeling the drizzle splatter against my skin. Lights from Salem played off the underside of the rain-gorged clouds.

Back in the house, I slipped into the laundry room and retrieved a towel to wipe Tessa's fur and my own feet. The cold settled into my bones, creating a nagging ache.

I checked the hall closet and found the bedding I would need. Throwing together a makeshift bed, I lied down and promptly fell asleep. Gregg's eyes danced in front of me, the dimple in his cheek deepening with his smile. Spicy tendrils of aftershave tickled my nose and the sensation of soft warm lips on mine had me moaning in my sleep.

Violent shaking woke me from my dream.

"Lucy! Lucy!"

I scrunched my eyes tighter. This had to be a nightmare trying to intrude into the ecstasy of my dream. If I ignored the noise, Gregg would return.

"Lucy!"

The urgency of the voice triggered goose flesh down my arms. Slowly opening an eye, the vision to greet me stopped my heart.

Cassie, dark circles under her eyes, stood over me, worry evident in every plane of her face.

I'd never noticed the tiny radiating wrinkles around her eyes. Good Lord, there was one, no two, wrinkles across her normally flawless forehead.

"What?!" I managed to croak out.

Cassie's eye and forehead wrinkles lessened. She blew out a breath.

I scrunched up my nose. "Whew girl. You need a mint. Why in the hell did you wake me up?"

She threw me a withering look. "You..." she pointed a finger at me. "...woke me up clear in the back of the house with your shouting."

I felt my cheeks burn.

"Uhmm. What was I yelling?"

She plopped down at the end of the couch, laying her head on the back cushion and closing her eyes.

"You were screaming Gregg's name and moaning '*No. Oh god, no.*' "

I felt moisture trickle down my cheek.

"Dammit!" I swiped at the tear.

Cassie lifted her head in time to see me wipe away the tear. She moved to my end of the couch and gathered me in her arms.

Oh, great! That's going to do it!

I burst into tears. I couldn't stop my sobbing. Raw emotions, just barely under check for years, now lay exposed in the open. My heart ached deep in my chest. This moment brought back the feeling of the day after… a day I'd tried to forget for over thirty years.

Cassie murmured into my hair. "It's okay, Lucy, it's okay."

After a very long five minutes, I found myself sucking in deep draughts of air and shuddering with each release.

"Okay, where is this jerk who caused you so much pain? I'll kick his ass from here to Hong Kong and back."

Shaking my head, I pulled Tessa closer and began absently stroking her fur.

"Can't do it."

"And why the hell not?" Worry had been replaced by explosive fury. "I've never seen you cry, let alone with this much pain evident. I'll kill the son-of-a…"

I put my hand up.

"When I tell you the rest of the story, you'll understand."

Cassie rose from the couch.

"Well, I sure as hell can't sleep now. I'm going to make some coffee and you're going to finish your story. I need to know what happened now more than ever."

I watched her stomp to the kitchen and lay my head against the padded arm of the divan. Tessa rolled her eyes to look at me. She slipped out her tongue and snuck a quick kiss across my chin.

I let a sad smile flash across my lips. I couldn't scold her now when she'd given me such comfort with one forbidden movement. I leaned over to kiss her forehead.

"What would I do without you?"

Her black tail thumped happily.

I'd closed my eyes and was beginning to drift into sleep when the clatter of cups and saucers jostled my peace.

"There is no way you're sleeping if I can't." Cassie had brewed a pot of coffee and poured it into a thermos along with all the makings, which she ferried to the living room. Leftovers from the night before were shoved to one side of the coffee table and the tray settled in the center.

By the time she finally poured the coffee into her mug, the resulting tan liquid bore no resemblance to the bitter concoction introduced by the Spaniards. Before settling completely on the floor, she retrieved a couple blankets from the hall closet.

Ten minutes of fussing and her likeness to a hen on a nest was amazing; blankets encased her, pillows fluffed beneath her and a half-closed-eye expression settled on her face.

I figured two minutes of talking would put her out.

"If you have any idea of trying to lull me to sleep and slink out of this, think again."

Snugging Tessa to my side, her warmth penetrating my clothes, I took a swallow of my coffee.

"Where was I?"

Cassie sipped her concoction.

"On the way back from the coast."

"Right. Well, we meandered back to the car…"

Chapter Twelve

1980

A sense of security enveloped me as we drove through the wooded cathedral of the Van Duzer corridor.

The warmth in the car precluded all talking. Words seemed-- unnecessary. As the forest bled into farmland, familiar pangs of doubt started attacking my serenity. Apparently, Gregg was experiencing the same sensations. We passed the Country Store in Grand Ronde before either of us spoke.

"How do you want to handle us, Lucy?"

I swiveled in my seat and took in his strong profile. What I wanted to do was shout to the world I'd finally fallen in love. Our months of sashaying around each other had produced the sensation for which everyone searched; a warm fuzzy feeling I identified as love. I sure as hell didn't want to give it up, but common sense prevailed.

"What I want to do and what we *should* do are day and night different. I think, at this point, we need to be cautious. You and I both know how vicious the rumor mill can be. I'm not sure about you, but I need my job."

Gregg agreed. "I'd love to retire but that's going to happen in about twenty-five years, not now. So Lucy? What next?"

The valley between the hills surrounding Grand Ronde disappeared past the car windows as we sped toward Salem.

"I think we need to keep up the facade of work buddies. There are those--people--who would do everything in their power to destroy any relationship we might attempt."

Gregg reached out his hand and gently stroked my cheek.

"I'll try but it's going to be damned hard, Lucy."

I looked into those amazing blue eyes.

"What?"

"I'm falling for you… falling hard."

My heart slammed against my chest. Suddenly all the air in the car had evaporated. An uninvited tear meandered down my cheek as I smiled.

"Me, too."

He swiped the tear from my cheek and flashed me his million-dollar smile.

We made the turn to Highway 18 on the last leg of the journey home.

I let my imagination play a few happily-ever-after scenarios but snapped back to the present when we had to stop at the traffic light outside Dallas. I needed to make a realistic decision.

"Let's continue to keep our day-to-days the same. We can always talk on the phone after work and maybe every other week we can go to the coast or spend a day in Portland."

His face took on a thoughtful look.

"Sounds like a good idea, but I already know I want more. It's taken me this long to ask you out because I was testing a theory."

"Oh?"

He cleared his throat as his face flushed a deep red.

"Yeah. I've watched the mating dance at the bar for a while. When Bob bought Lucky's, he let me move over there from the Red Goose. The game playing upped several notches. Stakes increased as did the payoffs.

"One of the more blatant moves I've noticed is the physical aspect of things. If a guy doesn't make a move by the third time the couple is together, the gals walk away. I'm not sure why exactly, but I've seen more couples breakup after the third date than I've seen lone wolves on the prowl. What's going on?"

I tried not to chuckle, but it bubbled up my throat causing him to frown.

"What's so funny?"

I stopped giggling but the smile never left my face.

"I'm afraid some fool male made the comment he liked aggressive women. The information pipeline being what it is had this bit of news around town in less than a week. Girls went from shy wallflowers to chandelier swingers overnight.

"I *think* I know who the culprit was. The ironic consequence of his brazen statement was a week after he pronounced his attraction to aggressive women, he fell head-over-heels in love with a shy, demure virgin; one of the very few I ever knew who had the right to wear white on her wedding day."

I snickered. "By that time the dye was cast. What you see out there is a generation of overly aggressive women hell bent on getting exactly what they want. I think you'll notice the guys getting dumped are the nice ones.

"The scoundrels and good-for-nothing creeps are cleaning up. Seems 'the badder-the-better' is the battle cry."

We were entering the city limits of West Salem.

He shook his head.

"Why do women do that to themselves?"

I gazed at the silver ribbon of water paralleling the road.

"Because they don't really know what they want."

"But why…"

I shrugged, the sadness of the truth tingeing my answer.

"Some people will try anything to reach the goal of what they *think* they want. It takes a brave soul to walk her own path around here. If you say no to the herd mentality, jealous people will still spread the lie you followed the crowd."

Waiting for the light to change on Commercial Street, Gregg stole a look at me.

"Sounds like the voice of experience."

I nodded my head ever-so-slightly.

"There's a very good reason why I choose to be on the working side of the bar. Once burned, twice shy."

We drove through town in silence, reality closing in around us. We made most of the lights through town and were only a block from my apartment when our good fortune ran out and the light turned red. As Gregg eased the car to a stop, I glanced to the little sports car stopping next to us.

Ducking to the floor, I fumbled with my purse.

"Lucy?"

"Hmmm?"

"What are you doing?"

I turned my head sideways to look his direction.

"If you'll *casually* look at the car next to us, you'll see Misty in the driver's seat." My cheek rested on the top of my knees. I watched his eyes flick sideways and heard the muttered swear word.

"Sorry about this, Luce."

Just before he turned up the volume on the radio, I heard his name being yelled.

The guitars blaring from the rock station screamed into my skull. I clenched my eyes shut and covered my ears with my hands, hoping the light would quickly change to green. The car lurched forward and I felt the acceleration of the engine. Gregg reached over and turned off the radio.

As I started to straighten up, he placed his hand on my back.

"Not quite yet. She's following me. I'm going to try and lose her on the back streets."

Having my head below my waist was affecting my equilibrium, and the erratic rolling back and forth of the car had me feeling I was about to lose the great lunch we'd had at Moe's. The scenery out his window gave me no clue as to where we were.

"Hold on."

The car screeched and tilted. I clutched the bottom of the seat and pinched my eyes closed. Abruptly, the vehicle jerked to a stop.

"Don't move, yet."

My heart thudded, breath coming in ragged gasps.

"I think I lost her. You can get up now."

I lifted my head to find we were in the parking lot of my apartment.

"Man, you're good."

He smirked. "If you only knew..."

Chapter Thirteen

He sat in his car, eyeing the staircase. She might be able to avoid the parking lot, but she had to climb the stairs to get to her apartment. Black steel glistened in the dying daylight. He stroked the barrel lovingly, the action releasing the subtle allusion of acrid metal cleaner beneath the oiled surface. Hours had been spent working on the tool, the result showing in the high gleam reflecting the pale illumination from beyond the car's windows.

His reverie was interrupted by a car, traveling entirely too fast, screeching into a space. The lights were flicked off and the driver sat immobile behind the wheel.

He took in the new model Chevrolet, the fancy wheels and tires, and felt a tingling sensation at the back of his scalp. He knew this car. But from where?

Before he could contemplate where he'd seen the car, she appeared at the passenger's side. She walked around and leaned down to the now opened driver's window. A male figure he recognized appeared and the two kissed.

This won't do. She's my diamond. No one is allowed to despoil my precious jewel.

He wrapped his hand around the solid metal base, his finger easily finding the trigger. Scrunching low in the seat, the visitor brought up the

9mm Browning and took careful aim at the dark-haired figure in the Chevrolet. He lined up the barrel, the occupant's temple coming into his sights.

"POW! You're dead."

~ * ~

The back of my neck prickled. Someone was watching; someone close. I squeezed Gregg's hand.

"I really hate to but I have to go. I'd invite you in but…"

He grinned. "Maybe later."

He pulled out of the parking space and, giving a quick wave, left.

I stood in the lot watching him turn onto the road and drive away, a contended sigh escaping my lips. Another prickle snaked up my spine. *Someone is watching me.* I whirled around trying to spot something, anything out of place. All I could see were empty cars in the lot. Shivering to my toes, I trotted to the stairs and bolted up the steps to my apartment. The glow of the day was still with me and I didn't want to let it go. I'd have to face the real world tomorrow. Tonight, I'd relive the best parts of the day with hot chocolate and television.

I turned to lock the door and the sensation of being watched tingled my scalp. I quickly turned the lock and slid the chain bolt into place. I couldn't shake the impression my movements were being monitored, so I closed every curtain and locked all my outer doors.

I needed to get over this silly feeling. I shook myself from head to toe. "There. Done. A hot shower will warm me up and get rid of this silly being-watched notion."

I grabbed a towel and headed to the bathroom.

~ * ~

He glanced up and down the breezeway before leaning his body against the door. The click of the lock snapped in his ear, chain rattling into place. *Good. She's settling in for the night.* He wouldn't have to stand watch. On tennis-shoed feet, he stole down the steps to his vehicle. His diamond, his Lucy would be secure tonight. If she left, he'd know. He'd placed a match on the sidewalk outside her door. She'd not be able to leave without breaking it in two. Before he went to work in the morning, he'd stop by and see if the unbroken match survived the night.

She was proving to be very difficult to protect. He could guard her place and watch her back when he knew where she was but this slip up... he was angry she'd escaped right under his nose. And with... *him*. The one who would hurt and leave her a wounded, crushed flower unfit for any man.

Richard growled deep in his throat. He unlocked his car, slipping behind the wheel, and sat staring at the light in her window. *Can't she see how bad he is for her? What will it take?*

Unconsciously, his hand found the Browning, which he cradled against his chest.

"I have your back, Lucy. You can count on me." His finger squeezed the trigger, the clacking of the hammer making him jump. He tossed the gun to the seat and started the car.

He would do his best to protect her, but she needed to see the error of her ways. Somehow he'd bring her around. Somehow...

Chapter Fourteen

2011

I looked up to find Cassie with her head against the couch cushion, eyes closed. Slowly, I rose from my spot.

"I'm not sleeping. Don't get any wild ideas about stopping now." She opened one eye and glared.

"I have to use the bathroom. Is that alright with you?"

"Fine. I could use the break myself. I'll use the one in my room; you can use the hallway facilities."

"Gee, thanks, mom."

Lifting her head up, she glowered as she shed the layers of blankets.

Once we took care of our business and returned, I continued.

"This next part I learned later through various other sources. If I had known back then, maybe…"

"Lucy--stop. Hindsight is *always* 20-20."

I huffed a big breath. "Here goes."

~ * ~

"Come on, come on!" The slight figure tapped a finger on the side of the phone. "Answer your phone." The ringing on the other end continued unabated.

"'Lo?" A baritone voice slurred.

"Gregg? You need to come get me at the train station."

Silence met the demand.

"I know you're still there, come get me!"

"Fine. Give me fifteen minutes. I'm, I *was*, sleeping you know. It is, after all, my day off."

"Just come get me. It's creepy and everybody is leaving. Mine was the last train of the night."

"On my way."

The tiny blonde moved to the window, clutching her overnight bag to her chest. Why was it, train stations were always in the darkest parts of the town? She jumped at the clacking sound of the grate being pulled across the doorways to the tracks.

A porter dressed in gray appeared at her right side.

"I'm sorry, miss, but you're going to have to wait outside. We're closing the station for the evening."

She stared at him, eyes wide, mouth hanging open.

"You're joking, right?"

He shook his head.

She ran a hand over her hair then stomped outside into the cool night air. The moment she stepped out of the building, the aroma of food wafted past her nose, her stomach reacting loudly.

She considered her position.

I can stand here and wait until he decides to show up or I can go over there and get something to eat.

There was no choice. She picked up her small valises and started toward the restaurant across the street from the college. She hadn't gone more than two feet when a car drove between her and her target. The passenger door opened.

"Get in."

"But…"

"Now."

She pushed the seat forward and tossed her bags in the back. When she'd adjusted her skirt, she slammed the door.

"I'm starved. I haven't eaten since before I left Seattle."

"There's food at the house."

"But that restaurant…"

"…is full of college boys willing to cause more trouble than I want to handle tonight."

"Gregg!"

"Audrey, we'll talk about it later. You woke me from a sound sleep. Once we get to the house, you can take your own car and get food if you're so determined. Right now, I just want to get home."

She crossed her arms over her chest and glared out at the road.

"Fine."

~ * ~

Gregg figured by the time she settled in for a few moments, exhaustion would take over and she'd wander to her bedroom and sleep for the next twelve hours. He was counting on it.

"How'd your visit go?"

He turned to look at the back of her blonde head.

"Audrey?"

"How do you think? Just like every other visit, it was a total disaster. There's no pleasing that woman."

"I think you're being too hard on her. After all, she only has your best interests at heart."

"Spare me the well-rehearsed pep talk. She's a selfish, self-centered…"

"Don't. I know the two of you don't get along but she and I do. Save your breath. We're home."

After parking and unloading the luggage, the pair went their separate ways once inside the small house. Gregg was tempted to pick up the phone and call Lucy just to hear her voice but stopped himself. The last thing he needed was to have Audrey get wind of the situation. He'd never hear the end of it and if she so much as breathed a word...

He shuddered and ambled into his bedroom to resume his sleep, hopefully. He heard the doors of the closet down the hall being slammed shut and a couple thuds on the floor. Within the next few minutes the only sounds reaching his ears was the ticking of his alarm clock.

Gregg smiled. Exhaustion was champion again. Sliding under the covers, his mind raced over the day's events a smile touching his lips. The future was looking very bright.

~ * ~

The closed door muffled the soft snoring, but Audrey knew Gregg wouldn't waken any time soon. She wasn't in the mood to sleep. The city called to her and with Gregg sleeping the night away... the town was hers to explore. She'd heard him talk about a few places and she wanted first hand experience not available to her if he was awake.

Patting her small purse, a sly smile touched her lips as she quietly closed and locked the front door. She sprinted to her car and drove to her first destination.

Stepping from the elevator, her stomach roiled.

"I know, I know. Just act like you do this every day and no one will be the wiser."

Several attractive young men tracked her as she walked past, putting a satisfied smile on her lips. Oh, yeah. *This is going to be fun.* She sat at the bar.

A pause in the music provided the bartender an opportunity to speak. "What'll it be, miss?"

She turned charcoal grey eyes the direction of the voice.

"White wine."

"ID, please."

She put the small purse on the bar top and pulled out the identification, sliding the driver's license to the dark haired, slender bartender.

Willow looked at the card and the young lady who'd handed it to her. She seemed unsure, but…

"One white wine coming up."

Audrey pulled out a five-dollar bill and placed it on the bar. She turned to watch the action on the dance floor. Gregg hadn't said anything about how much fun this was. All he did was complain about the noise and drunks.

A lanky man, gold chains sparkling in the disco ball's glittering light, swaggered to her chair.

"Hey, baby. Wanna dance?"

Audrey let her eyes survey him head to toe. Good clothes, expensive jewelry and an overabundance of ego. Leaning back a little in the barstool, she observed a table of guys whispering and nudging each other, their lascivious grins evident across the room.

She didn't say anything.

"Well?" He was beginning to shift his weight from foot to foot.

"Thanks, but no." She turned to take a sip of her wine.

"Why not?" He stepped toward her.

Audrey whipped around. "Because I said no."

He backed up. "No need to get uptight, baby. Just thought I'd do you a favor."

She let the hint of a smile touch the corner of her mouth. "Don't bother."

His mouth turned down as he gave her the once over. "Bitch." He stomped back to the table of guys.

She watched him shake his head and couldn't help the smile spreading across her face.

"Be careful."

Audrey looked up to find the bartender putting change in front of her drink.

"What?"

"Don is arrogant and doesn't often get told no."

Audrey tilted her head. "There's always a first time, isn't there?"

"He can be pretty vicious."

"Thank you for the head's up, but I'm very picky about my companions. He isn't even close to my type."

Willow smiled. "Good. Just checking." She extended her hand. "I'm Willow."

Audrey grasped the proffered appendage. "Audrey."

"I know."

"I've not seen you around. New to town?"

"Yeah. Just getting my bearings. I've been listening to the chatter among my co-workers. I'm checking out the action a little at a time."

Willow looked over her shoulder to the clock on top of the register.

"Whoops. Time to start shutting down. Welcome to town, Audrey. Just be careful of the wolves." She headed to the end of the bar where the cocktail waitresses had been piling up the empty glasses.

Audrey finished her wine and waved at Willow as she headed toward the exit. She stood waiting for the elevator, distress invading her senses when four young men stumbled into the hallway.

"Hey, Don. Here's your opportunity to try again."

The tall brunette stumbled her direction.

Audrey frantically searched for an escape, spotted the door to the restroom and dashed inside locking herself into one of the stalls. The door creaked open. Carefully placing her feet on the back of the toilet seat, she squatted down and held her breath.

"Oh, my god! Did you see Don making a fool of himself over that new blonde at the bar? What an idiot! She doesn't look old enough to be in the restaurant let alone the bar."

Audrey blew out the breath she was holding but kept her position, hoping she could get a little inside information for free.

"Well, she looks like trash to me."

There was a noise Audrey could only guess as a huff.

"Misty, you think every pretty girl is trash."

She thinks I'm pretty. A grin covered the hideaway's face.

"Just as long as she stays away from Gregg, we'll be doing okay. He's mine. I don't care what anyone else thinks; I'll have that man if it kills me. He's going to be worth a ton of money some day and I'll be there to help him spend it. Besides, I think we'd make pretty kids."

A groan echoed through the nearly empty restroom.

"Quit dreaming, Misty. He doesn't even like you. I've never seen him make eyes at anybody. Maybe he's gay. Let's go to Denny's. I'm starving."

"Well, you drive, 'cause I'm too drunk."

The voices faded and Audrey tenuously placed her feet on the floor. She slid the latch open and peeked into the mirror facing the stalls. No one was in the bathroom. She maneuvered her way into the elevator hallway. In less than twenty minutes, the roar of music and chattering patrons had stilled to unearthly quiet. There was the faint clinking of glassware and she could only guess the bartenders and waitresses were cleaning up for the night. Otherwise, the top floor of the building sounded and felt deserted.

When the elevator bell rang, she jumped and clutched at her chest. Entering the silver-lined room, she pushed the button, her heart racing until the doors closed.

Where did I park?

Once in the main lobby, her wits sharpened and she quick-stepped to her vehicle.

The next step was slipping inside Gregg's place without being caught. After that, it was a downhill ride.

She parked in her designated spot and quietly entered the house. As she leaned against the front door, she sighed. *Safe.*

"Where the hell were you?"

"Aaaahhhh!" Audrey jumped and dropped her purse. "You scared me."

The overhead light illuminated the room with a brilliance she hadn't recalled.

72

"Really? Imagine my feelings when I woke up and checked on you to find the room empty. Where the hell were you?" Gregg's face was crimson.

Audrey could see him quaking in anger. She picked up her purse and looked him in the eye.

"None of your business." The minute the words left her lips she knew it was the wrong thing to say. His face deepened in color and the quaver she'd witnessed turned into visible shaking.

"As long as you live in my house, you'll go by my rules. Are we clear?"

"You're not my..." she had the good sense to stop before adding fuel to the fire. "Fine. I'm going to bed." Starting to stomp toward her room, her progress was stopped by an arm blocking the way.

"Not until you give me the key to the house."

She whipped around to face him. "WHAT!"

Sensing a major argument about to explode, Gregg dropped his arm.

"We'll continue this later this morning."

Audrey continued her stalk to her room and slammed the door.

Gregg sighed and crawled back into bed.

This situation was not turning out how he'd hoped.

Chapter Fifteen

I looked in the mirror and smiled. It was really hard not to after the day Gregg and I had spent together. That man was so unlike any I'd ever met before, I was finding it hard to keep my perspective.

"Take a deep breath, Lucy." One last brush stroke through my hair and I was ready. My emotions were jumbled; I felt uncertain about the night ahead. The one constant throughout my chaotic life had always been my job. Behind the bar, I had *some* control of the happenings in my space. Now my mind was occupied with thoughts of Gregg.

Stepping on a match in front of my door after I'd locked the apartment, I muttered something about piggy neighbors and hurried down the steps, taking them two at a time. The drive to work passed quickly and I was soon deep into the opening routine of the night shift. After making sure all the waitresses had their banks and station assignments, I leaned against the counter for the first time in two hours.

Willow rang up an order on the register then turned to me. "Welcome back. How was it?"

I tried my best to be enigmatic but couldn't contain the bubble of happiness filling my heart. I broke into a wide smile. "Amazing."

Willow's eyes widened. "Wow. I've never heard you use that word about a guy--ever."

I started to answer her but was interrupted by the cocktail waitress waving an order.

"We'll talk later."

Thursday nights started slow, but around ten or so went into overdrive. Every bar in town featured Thursday as Ladies' Night and the patrons used it as an excuse to kick off the weekend. If you enticed the ladies through the door, the men would soon follow. About eleven thirty or so, a beautiful, lissome blonde who appeared too young to be in the bar caught my eye.

I caught Willow's attention. Trying to communicate over the pounding of the music blasting from the speakers was proving difficult, so I motioned to her to meet me in the cooler.

Cool air enveloped me providing a relief from the hot, smoky atmosphere behind the bar. Willow wrapped her arms around herself.

"Jiminy, Lucy. What's so important you pulled me into here?"

"Did you see the slim blonde at the end of the bar?"

"Which one?"

"Sitting on the corner facing the dance floor. She's wearing skintight straight leg jeans and a light colored peasant blouse. She doesn't look old enough to be in here. Did you card her?"

Willow pinned a look on me so fierce I was afraid she was going to punch me.

"Are you doubting my ability as a bartender? Because if you are, I can go to Lucky's and start tomorrow." She turned on her heel and shoved open the door.

I chased after her but she was elbow deep in orders with her back to me. I looked at my order rack and proceeded to start on the half dozen orders waiting my attention. When the music had cooled, I ventured to her end of the bar.

"Listen…"

She held up a hand.

I was afraid she was going to tell me to take a hike but she pulled in a deep breath and turned to me.

"I'm sorry, Lucy. Your question just struck me wrong. She was in here last night and I checked her ID, but you couldn't have known that. You were too busy falling in love."

"What?!" I watched her eyes twinkle in the lights. "I'm not..."

She broke out laughing. "Don't try to deny it. The minute I asked you about yesterday, your face lit up and you started smiling. That man has you by the heartstrings."

She wiggled her eyebrows at me then I watched the mirth disappear from her face. Willow leaned to me and spoke in my ear.

"The Strange One just walked in. He's at your end of the bar." Turning around, she hurried to her drink well to fill orders.

I pulled in a measured breath and pasting a smile on my face headed to my station.

"Richard, nice to see you. How are you tonight?"

His eyes swept over me and his mouth turned downward. "You weren't here yesterday. I didn't see your car downstairs."

"That's right, Richard. I get two days a week off and yesterday was one of those days."

"What did you do?"

I looked up into angry blue eyes.

"Richard? Can I get you anything?"

Narrowing his gaze at me, I watched his jaw muscle work.

"No. You can't be protected if you won't listen." He turned and stomped out the door.

"What was that all about?"

I jumped. Willow had come up behind me while I was concentrating on keeping Richard from flipping out and causing a scene.

"You scared me."

"That's about the fastest I've seen him come and go out of here. What'd he say to you?"

I turned to see the waitress at her end of the bar waving an order in the air.

"Let's talk after we close."

"Deal."

The next two hours flew by and soon we were chasing the last stragglers from the bar out the door.

Banks counted and dropped in the safe, we sat sorting our tips as we sipped on our shift drinks.

Willow folded her currency and put it in the blue bag with gold trim she carried just for the occasion. "Fill me in on The Strange One's visit tonight."

I slugged back a shot followed by a cola chaser. "Apparently he's keeping tabs on me."

Willow lifted one brow. "Oh? What do you mean by *keeping tabs*?"

I went around the bar and poured myself another shot.

"He told me he can't protect me if I won't listen. A couple nights ago when I was leaving to go home, he showed up. Scared the hell out of me. The next morning when Gregg came over, he brought in a note and a rose. I thought it was such a sweet thought until he told me he couldn't take credit for it. The card and flower were on the door when he arrived.

"Needless to say, my skin crawled when I realized who put those things on my door. *My door*, Willow. This guy knows where I live."

I started shaking and a tear meandered down my cheek. "I won't lie. I'm scared. What the hell am I going to do?"

Willow put an arm around me. "Gosh, Lucy. I don't know what to tell you. Have you called the police?"

I looked at her. "And tell them what? I have an admirer I'm scared of? They'd laugh at me or tell me to feel lucky. He's just this side of being really creepy."

Squeezing my shoulders gently, she smiled. "You can always come and stay with me."

"Thanks, but if I do that, then he wins, doesn't he? And to be truthful with you, I don't want to be chased from my home."

"Listen, it's getting late and I'm beginning to feel my eyelids dropping to my knees. I want a few details about yesterday. Give. How was it?"

I leaned back against the bar stool and let the warm glow of the day wash over me.

"Amazing... absolutely amazing. We talked and laughed and I swear we stopped at every tourist trap in Lincoln City."

"Did you stop at Moe's?"

"Please." I rolled my eyes skyward. "Going to the coast and not stopping at Moe's is like going to the coast and not getting salt water taffy."

"Yeah! By the way, where's mine?"

I grabbed my purse and rummaged inside pulling out a small wax-coated white container. "You mean this?"

I handed her the bag and watched her eyes light up as she licked her lips.

"Oooo, my dentist will kill me."

"Excellent. Then my mission here is complete. Let's go home. Tomorrow will come soon enough."

We cleaned up our glasses and made sure the top of the bar was wiped down. Willow, being the last to leave, flipped off the lights and left the room in darkness.

We chatted about the night's business in the elevator and parted at the first floor. I'd been just a bit too late to secure a parking spot beneath the building so was forced to put my car in the bank's lot next door. Once inside my vehicle, as I sat waiting for the heater to warm, the skin on my arms prickled. I whipped my head around looking in all directions but couldn't spot anything out of the ordinary. Still, chills traveled my spine. I jammed the car in gear and sped from the lot onto the main road. As early as it was in the morning, there were a surprising number of cars on the streets. Though my heart was pounding with fear and all I wanted to do was be in my safe home, I stopped at all the lights and kept my foot from jamming the gas pedal to the floor. No sense in getting a ticket.

I darted up the stairs. When I'd pushed my way inside and bolted the door, I finally breathed. What was I going to do? I didn't want to spend all my life looking over my shoulder and the police would just laugh at me.

I'd love to hear the sound of Gregg's warm voice telling me I was being silly. If only…

I sighed and began the process of unwinding. Unlike my usual nighttime routine of reading for several hours, I dropped into bed completely exhausted. Deep, dark sleep overtook my thoughts and chased the concerns of the day from my mind.

~ * ~

2011

I glanced up at Cassie, still resembling a nesting hen, and commented quietly.

"I promise I'll finish the rest of the story but right now, I'm utterly exhausted. I need to sleep, girlfriend."

She humphed and started to unscramble her legs.

"Fine, but if I have to pay for more landscaping to get you to tell me the whole story, I'll re-landscape the city of Silverton if necessary. I *will* find out why I can't black the eye of someone who's caused you so much pain."

She left the nest and padded back to her room, ignoring the tiny slip of pink coloring the horizon outside the windows. I nudged Tessa and we both trotted to the bedroom to give this sleeping thing another shot. I could only surmise the next part of the story because I hadn't actually been present for the activities until *that* night. I really needed to get some rest because I wasn't sure I could hold back the tears any longer to finish my story. I pulled up the covers and snugged my dog next to me, slipping into dark bliss with her warmth against my body.

Chapter Sixteen

Five hours later, my troubled sleep interrupted by a cold, wet anxious nose, we completed the perfunctory morning walk and I fed Tessa. While rummaging in the kitchen cupboards for breakfast makings, I realized a trip into town was a necessity unless I was going to make reheated pizza my meal of choice. I wasn't.

It must have been the smell of cooking food that roused Cassie from her sleeping cave because it sure wasn't the glorious sunshine. Lightly clouded but bright, spring was still being fickle and cool. She stumbled in, her slippers shushing against the tiling and, with eyes half closed, poured a cup of fresh brewed coffee. The doctored results produced a thin smile of satisfaction. Plopping her thin frame at the breakfast bar, she sat staring through the magnificent picture window, but I doubt she saw the greenery beyond.

I set a plate of food in front of her and watched as she inhaled the contents.

"More?"

"Sure." This was one of the traits I hated about Cassie--she could eat her weight in food and not gain a pound. Oh, well. I created another omelet complete with toast for her and myself and sat at the bar. Once I was finished, she rose from her chair and cleaned the kitchen, popping the dirty kitchenware into the dishwasher.

She poured and doctored another cup of coffee and, with a motion of her forefinger, directed me to follow her to the living room.

We settled into our respective places.

"I know you thought I might forget about the rest of the story but I haven't. Lucy, please continue." Cassie sipped her brew.

"Well, I don't plan on spending my one long weekend inside your magnificent house rehashing my past so I'm going to cut to the meat of the story and finish before this evening. Then you're going to take me to a fantastic restaurant after which time we'll head to the best dance spot in town for someone my age. I'm going to proceed to get roaring drunk, and you'll get the pleasure of taking care of me tomorrow when my head is splitting and my stomach is roiling."

"And why is that?"

"If you're dragging me through the worst hell of my life, there had better be a reward at the end of this exercise." I looked up from my cup at Cassie.

"Deal. Let's get going."

"Okay. To the best of my recollection…"

~ * ~

1980

Time passes quickly during the holidays and Gregg and I stole what days off we could, leaving town to spend time together. A few co-workers seemed to understand we were dating and, thankfully, they'd opted to keep quiet about our relationship. We'd started seeing each other at the end of summer. By the time Halloween rolled around, I knew I was irretrievably in love with him. He was all I could think about and not being able to talk with my friends about us was taking its toll on me.

With annoying frequency Misty, the bar troublemaker, had started slinking to my side of the bar and gossiping about a beautiful blonde hanging around Gregg.

"I swear, Dee Dee, every time I go past his house, she's coming out the door. I mean, if she's not his live-in, who is she?" Misty shot me a look.

Wisely, I didn't raise my head and give her the satisfaction of seeing me flinch. I could see the nasty smirk on her face in the mirror.

"Misty, I have no idea. Let's just get a drink and circulate. I see that gorgeous Steve over there by himself. He owns a Corvette I'm going to be riding in by the end of the night. Come on." Dee Dee grabbed her drink from the bar and moved toward her quarry.

Looking up, I caught the sour expression on Misty's face. She was determined to one-up me. Problem is a person has to want to be one-upped for the action to count. I filled a drink order and wandered to Willow's side.

"It's taking everything in my power not to come across the bar and wipe the smirk off Misty's face but you know what?"

Willow shook her head as she pulled a new bottle of bar vodka from beneath her sink.

"She's really hit a sore spot. I know the holidays are busy, but it seems lately every time Gregg and I make plans, he calls thirty or forty minutes before we're supposed to go out and cancels."

She turned. "Maybe he's being called into work more often. Come on, Lucy, you've been in this business long enough to know the holidays are when people bail on their jobs. Most first-timers don't want to work Halloween, Thanksgiving or Christmas. They've not been around long enough to realize that's when you make the best tips."

We were both being hailed by customers and had to discontinue our conversation, but I grasped at Willow's positive take on the situation. I needed to be hopeful. Having my heart broken again was not in my game plan.

Twenty minutes after the short rush of orders, I looked up into the lifeless eyes of the Strange One.

"Richard. I didn't see you."

"She's right, you know." He stared at me.

"Who's right?" I was loading glasses into my dishwasher.

"The mean girl. I've been watching him…"

I snapped my head up and glared.

"…and the blonde girl is with him, a lot. She also goes out to other bars and dances with other men when he's working. I don't think he likes it cause I've heard him yell at her about it."

"Richard, I have no idea what you're talking about." Slamming the door of the dishwasher shut, I started the cycle, the noise drowning out further conversation.

He stood waiting, watching me the entire time.

"He's going to hurt you, Lucy. Mark my words." With that he turned and walked out of the bar.

I needed to find who was this blonde everyone was seeing with Gregg. Asking him directly was out of the question. After all, we were just dating.

The cloud started by Misty and built on by Richard hung over me the rest of the night. By the time we closed the bar, I was on the edge of insanity.

Willow prodded. "What's the problem?"

I shrugged my shoulders and vehemently scrubbed my side of the bar.

"LUCY!"

The sound caused me to jump and twirl around. Willow *never* raised her voice.

"Don't tell me nothing is wrong." She pulled out a bar stool and pointed to it. "Get over here and sit. We're not leaving this place until you tell me what's going on."

Obediently, I walked around the bar and took the chair she'd indicated.

"The Strange One was here tonight."

"I know. I saw him. You were fine until he left. What did he say to you? Did he threaten you?"

I shook my head. "No. He just verified what Misty has been saying. Gregg has been with some blonde--quite a bit. Seems she goes to his job as well as out on the town." I turned to Willow, a tear meandering down my cheek. "I--I can't get my heart broken again."

She tilted her head and ran her hand down my arm. "Sorry, friend. Seems as though it's already happened. However, don't believe *anything* Misty says and take what the Strange One says to you with a bucket of salt. You have to keep in mind, for whatever bizarre reason, he seems to feel like he's your protector."

I pulled in a stuttered breath. "Yeah, you're right but all of these broken dates are beginning to feel like a brush off."

"You want me to call him?"

"NO!"

Willow raised her eyebrows. "Why not?"

"Because I have to trust him to tell me the truth eventually. If I send someone to grill him now, he'll think I don't. That'll kill any hope of an honest relationship."

"Whatever you want. Just be careful how much you show here at work. If you act like you did the last half of tonight, you'll hand Misty the biggest gift of her life; the possibility you believe her."

I considered Willow's advise. "Got it. I'm sure everything will work out."

"Yep. Meanwhile, let's get the hell out of Dodge and go home. I'm tired and tomorrow is Saturday night. Going to be twice as busy as tonight."

I groaned. "Yeah. See you tomorrow."

The silence on the way home was eerie but I'd opted not to turn on the radio to give myself some quiet for thinking. By the time I turned out the lamp next to my bed, I'd come to a decision. I could only hope I wouldn't chicken out Monday.

Chapter Seventeen

Monday morning

I slugged down my coffee and grabbed the phone. If I didn't dial the number right now, I'd lose my nerve. The phone rang at the other end. If he didn't answer after six rings...

"Hello?"

Jumping, I sucked in a breath. "Gregg!"

"Yeah?"

"Sorry. This is Lucy."

"Oh, hey hon, it just didn't sound like you. What's up?"

"I feel like a complete idiot. I think I left my jean jacket in your car the last time we went to the zoo. How about I come over and pick it up? I'll need it after work tonight."

I could hear him breathing into the receiver. He was sure taking a long time to answer.

"Uh, sure."

"I'll just pop by and check in the car in about an hour. Will that work for you."

"Uhm, I guess that'll be fine. Come on over."

"Gregg?"

"Yeah?"

"I've never been to your house. You'll need to give me your address and directions."

"Really? In all the months we've been dating you've never been here?"

"Never."

"Well, I guess we'll just have to fix that."

He proceeded to give me the street address and directions from my apartment to his house.

"Thanks. I'll see you in an hour."

"See you, Lucy."

I almost felt guilty--almost. I had a plan I intended to implement as soon as I hung up. Getting my purse and leaving the apartment, I crawled in my car and headed to Gregg's. The traffic was light and I arrived earlier than I'd planned so drove up the lane, spotting the address and his car in the driveway. There was a cross street where I could park out of sight. I circled the block and moved my car to a spot where I had a straight line of vision to the front of the house.

I watched and hoped I was wasting my time. In the back of my mind I could hear Misty's obnoxious voice droning on about the gorgeous blonde flitting around Gregg. *She's wrong. He's explained why he's not been able to make our dates every time. Misty's just jealous.*

I smiled as my shoulders relaxed. Movement near the front of the house caught my attention. The door swung open and Gregg was escorting a lithe, blonde to the car parked near the curb. He had his arm slung across her shoulder and after he opened her door, he kissed her forehead. She slid into the driver's seat, Gregg closing the door and waving as the car pulled from the curb.

I could feel my heart breaking. I was being played and I didn't like the sensation anymore this time than the last. He walked across the lawn to the door and turned. I slid down the seat counting to twenty then peeked over the door ledge. The porch was empty.

"I'm done. I won't go through this again." Sobbing uncontrollably I started the car and raced home. I'd been so wrapped up in my own misery I'd blocked out everything around me, including the vehicle trailing me through the traffic.

~ * ~

He was driving past her apartment house on the way to the firing range, just making sure she was safely inside, when her car pulled in front of his. Backing off three vehicle lengths behind her, he noted she was heading toward town. The sky was still bright with sunshine so she couldn't be going to work. *If she continues to disregard my advice to stay inside her apartment, I can't protect her.* Well, guard her he would. He continued trailing her, losing sight of the vehicle once in South Salem and panicking until he saw the car coming toward him. He quickly reconnoitered the area and found a spot to turn around just as she disappeared around a corner. He raced to the street, noting she'd parked a few houses down against the curb. He zipped off a left turn in the path of an oncoming driver, incurring a hand sign and shouted obscenity then moved his vehicle close to the corner. He kept his eyes on her as she observed a house down the side street. Leaning forward, his sightline caught the tail end of a familiar car.

"So you're checking up on him. Maybe you'll believe me now." A rare smug smile spread over his face. He was being vindicated. She would *surely* come to him for comfort.

He tried as best he could to see what was happening, but the house was just too far away for him to get a good look at any action. What he could see of her reactions was not good. When she burst into tears, her shoulders shaking, and screeched from the curb, he was caught off guard.

"Damn you, Gregg. You've hurt her for the last time." He jammed his car into gear and tore after her. He didn't have to worry about keeping his distance this time because she was speeding through traffic, weaving across the lanes toward the north. He could only guess she was going home so he backed off and took the familiar backstreets to her apartments.

When he arrived, her vehicle was in its designated parking place and he chose a visitor spot to back into. He reached across the seat and unconsciously stroked the black case. When he surmised an hour had passed and she'd not come back out, he patted the case and left to get in some practice. His previous time at the range had been to keep his skills sharp. Now he had a mission.

"It's time for me to fight for the honor of my lady."

~ * ~

I ran blindly up the stairs, tears streaming down my cheeks, and slammed my door closed. Dashing into my bedroom, I threw myself on the bed and sobbed until my throat was raw and I had no more tears. *How could I have been so blind? God, Misty will be crowing for a month if she finds out how I'd let myself be duped. As far as I'm concerned, she can have him.*

The phone rang. Out of habit, I picked it up.

"Hello?"

"Lucy? Are you okay?"

The minute I heard his voice I wanted to slam down the receiver.

"Yeah, allergies that's all."

"I was beginning to get worried. It's half an hour after you said you'd be here. You're always on time."

I had to think quickly. "Oh, how stupid of me. I was going to call you back and let you know--I went through my closet again and found the jacket I thought I left in your car. Sorry."

"Hon? Are you sure you're okay? You sound… different."

I hadn't realized how brusque I'd come across on the phone.

"Fine. Just a bit rushed. Shortly after I found my jacket, Willow called and asked me to hit the shops with her. That must be her knocking, so I really have to go. I'll call you later. Bye, Gregg." I hung up before he could answer and the floodgates opened again.

I was glad I had tonight and tomorrow off. I'd need the time to get myself together.

Chapter Eighteen

The trigger clicked with a satisfying snap. The jerk of the gun in his hands and acrid smell of gunpowder in his nostrils set his head to spinning. He marched to the target and reached a finger to touch the hole in the dead center.

"This is for you, Lucy."

The only detail left was to decide the day of his mission, the one certainty being the necessity for swift justice. His lady Lucy was in pain and the cause required curing. He hummed on the drive home, parking his car next to the building.

Inside his unit, he stopped and shed his clothing. After placing the germ-laden items in the green garbage bag to be disposed of later, he donned clean underwear and padded to the kitchen to peer at the wall calendar. He'd have to go out tonight to verify his suspicions, but if they proved true, he knew exactly the day and time to make sure his Lucy would be safe forever.

"Hello?"

The click of the hang up was harsh but he understood.

"I'll make the world safe for you, my lady. It won't be long now."

~ * ~

I'd avoided answering the phone for several hours suspecting Gregg would try and contact me again. After four or five times of the blasted thing ringing and ringing, I finally answered the sixth call.

"Hello?"

Silence met my ears, only it wasn't the stillness of a hung up call. It was the quiet of a live person not speaking. I could hear breathing. Chills shot down my spine.

"Hello?" After the second attempt I hung up.

"I have no time for prank callers." I unplugged the darn thing from the wall.

"There. They can call all they like and I won't hear it and won't care."

Looking at the clock, a wave of guilt washed over me. I wasn't one to give in to illness and emotionality, but I knew I couldn't deal with other people right at this moment. Everything and everybody I was around reminded me of Gregg in one way or another. I definitely couldn't swing by his workplace tonight and watch him work. Not with the knowledge I'd recently acquired. My heart ached at the thought and unbidden tears streaked down my cheeks. Maybe by the time Ladies' Night rolled around on Thursday, I'd feel more confident about watching others hook up.

Right now I planned on watching television until my eyes exploded from my head.

~ * ~

He took one last look in the mirror and brushed a wayward strand of hair into place.

"Time to go."

With determination in his step, he left the apartment and headed to Lucky's. He walked through the door, flinching at the loudness of the jukebox music then sat at the end of the bar nearest the exit. He patted the rigid form in his pocket, the action calming his roiling stomach.

~ * ~

"What can I get you?" Gregg Halsey looked at the Strange One. He seemed unusually calm. A trait Gregg wouldn't have assigned to the man.

"Long neck. Please bring it here so I can open it."

"Of course."

Heading back to the cooler, Gregg felt uneasy. The Strange One was in the bar on a Monday. Not normal. And… he seemed to be watching more than what was right in front of him. Gregg reached in to grab the beer and peered sideways through the thick glass door. The man was reconnoitering the room and making notes on a small tablet. As soon as Gregg pulled the long necked bottle from the cooler, he noted the little book disappear from the top of the bar. Swiping the opener from the side of the cash register, he moved to the bar's end and placed bottle and opener in front of the Strange One.

"Here you go. That'll be $2.50."

The Strange One opened the bottle and took a swig. He retrieved his money and paid for the drink.

"How are Thursday nights here?"

Gregg was amazed. The man never instigated a conversation.

"Uhm. Hopping. It's Ladies' Night and we usually have a band."

"Think I might come in and watch the action."

"Sure. Lots of ladies." Gregg took the opener and walked back to the register to put the money inside. When he turned to take the change to the end of the bar, the beer was sitting there but not the man. He shivered to his toes. Something about this didn't feel right, but he couldn't put his finger on exactly what was wrong.

"Just my imagination." All day his mind had been playing games with him. Why, he even had the feeling Lucy was mad at him. *Can't be. I haven't done anything wrong.*

He was going to have to pop in on her. He'd tried calling several times before he went to work and her phone just rang and rang. She had said she and Willow were going shopping, but Lucy had told him more than once she hated all day shopping sprees.

"Maybe they went out to dinner." He looked up at his reflection in the mirror. "No. Willow works tonight 'cause it's Lucy's night off. Bet she had to cover for somebody. I'll try tomorrow. I know she's off again tomorrow."

"You lose something?" Lana, the only waitress for the evening, peered at him with arched brows.

Gregg smiled. "Just my mind."

"Figured that. See if you can find it and fill this order for me. Seems to be getting busier by the minute. Didn't anyone tell these people tomorrow is a work day?"

"Apparently not, but don't complain. More money in our pockets."

"True enough." She placed the drinks on her tray. "I'd keep the thinking out loud to a minimum. Those guys in the white coats are waiting around the corner, you know?" She winked as she walked away.

She's right. Before he could ruminate on his problem, several customers sat at the bar and the night kicked into gear. The band would start in an hour and communication would become all but impossible.

He needed to contact Lucy, face to face, as soon as possible.

~ * ~

My weekend, Monday and Tuesday, was interminable but I made it through. When Wednesday rolled around, I pulled myself together and went to work. The night was slow, as I'd expected, as not too many customers ventured out of their homes in the middle of the week. Willow and I chitchatted about the comings and goings of the bar crowd, who was an item and who was no longer dating. We were in the middle of the catch up when she nodded toward my end of the bar.

"You have a customer."

I turned and faced the tentative smile of the man I loved.

"I can't. Please take his order." I started to walk toward the restaurant when Willow caught my arm.

"He's seen you. Suck it up, Lucy, whatever it is, and serve the man. You owe him an explanation."

I snapped. "I owe him nothing. The last time I *sucked it up* and gave a man the opportunity to explain, he went on for two more years to shatter my self-esteem and trample on my heart. I owe nothing to anyone but myself."

She put her hand on my arm and with a touch gentled my anger. "Lucy, the man loves you. It's so evident I can see it from here. Those who don't see it don't want to. You owe it to yourself to talk with him." She pinned me with a look. "You're bigger than this. You can handle it."

I knew she was right but hated the process of learning to stand alone on my two feet again.

"Fine. But I'm *not* responsible for my mood afterward."

She smiled. "Yes, you are. You'll do fine. Now go." She nudged me toward the end of the bar.

I dragged my feet playing over in my mind what I might say.

"Hi, Lucy."

"Gregg. What can I get for you?"

His eyes radiated hurt. "So that's how we're going to do this? Lucy, what did I do? I've gone over everything in my mind from the last time we talked, and I can't remember what I did to upset you. Please talk to me."

I looked at the dark blue eyes crinkling in concern and turned to Willow.

"Taking a break. I'll be back in twenty."

She waved an arm at the barren tables. "Take your time, I think I can handle it."

I led the way to the quiet restaurant, Gregg following closely on my heels. We sat in a booth near the kitchen and faced each other.

I pulled in a deep breath. "I guess I owe you an explanation."

"That would be nice."

"Please let me say what I need to say before you add anything or interrupt."

"Deal."

"I went to your house last week to verify some pretty ugly rumors I'd been hearing in the bar."

He started to say something but stopped when I held up my hand.

"When I'm done."

He nodded his agreement.

"I was on a side street that offered a pretty good view of your house. Not long after I parked, you came out the front door and escorted a blonde to her car. You kissed her and went back inside." *There. I've said it.* "I can't abide liars and cheats. I made the mistake once of believing a man who did both. I won't do it again."

Several emotions crossed his face and he seemed to struggle for words.

"Whew, I know this looks really bad but there's a very good explanation for the blonde."

I lifted a brow. "I'd really be interested in hearing it." I crossed my arms and sat back in the comfortably padded booth.

"She's my sister."

Rolling my eyes, I spit out, "Come on, Gregg. You can do better than that."

He waited for a minute. "If it was a lie, sure, but I'm not lying Lucy. Can I explain?"

I shrugged my shoulders. "Be my guest."

He pulled in a deep breath and settled back into the cushion. "My parents are extreme religious zealots. I left home as soon as I could and struck out on my own. I have a sister, Audrey, who is as fair as I'm dark and twelve years younger. She stayed as long as she could handle the restrictions. She was acting out so much that after six years of no contact with me, my mom called and asked me if I would let Audrey come live with me. They figured her living with a family member was better than her living alone.

"I know she's been hitting some of the clubs in town and the problem with that is she's only twenty. Apparently, she has ID that shows her as twenty-three or twenty-four. I'm guessing what you saw the other day was me sending her off to Chemeketa for classes."

I searched his face in the darkened room for signs of deception and saw none. I swallowed. "I, uh, feel like an idiot. I, uh, I'm sorry."

Gregg held up a hand. "Not yet. If I were a really slick jerk I could come up with a story like that to suck you in but I want you to believe me."

He reached around and grabbed his wallet. Flipping it open he pulled out a couple photos and slid them to me.

"Here. This one," he moved a family photo my direction, "is right after Audrey was born. As you can see my parents are quite conservative."

I pulled over the lit candle and held up the picture. The man looked angry in his black suit and the woman was buttoned up to her chin. Her hair was caught up in some sort of white cap and she held a towheaded baby in her arms. The young man in the front looked miserable with his bowl haircut and Sunday suit.

"This was taken at the beginning of this year. I wanted something more current so we went to the Photography Shop for the pictures."

Sitting side by side slightly facing each other was Gregg and the blonde woman I saw him escort to the car. The difference was striking; she was as fair as he was dark but they shared a likeness of eyes and smile. There really was no doubt she must be related. I slid back the pictures.

"God, I feel like an idiot."

"Don't. I should have let you know about her sooner. I'd planned on it but when I started getting calls from some of my bartending buddies telling me she was out and about, I found myself caught up in trying to keep her from getting thrown out of the clubs before she was old enough to enter them. I guess I wasn't prepared to be a father quite yet."

He looked up at me through those full thick black lashes that rimmed his dark eyes.

"Please say we're okay?" He put out his hand, palm up, in invitation.

I worried my bottom lip and slid my hand into his. "Yes, if you'll forgive my stupidity."

"How can you be stupid if you love me?"

The twinkle in his eye was evident even in the dark room.

"You are a scoundrel, you know it?"

"And the problem with that is…?" He slid around to me and gathered me into his arms crushing my lips beneath his.

I felt my core explode into flames. His tongue teased my lips and I allowed him entry. The emotions raised by our kiss shut out the rest of the room. I could feel his warm breath on my cheek and my hands tangled in his silky locks. The muscles of his chest crushed me to him and I melted into his arms. This was exactly where I wanted to be.

I suspect we would have stayed locked in embrace all night if a busboy hadn't appeared at our table and cleared his throat.

"Excuse me, Lucy, but Willow says you need to get out front right now. She told me to tell you the Strange One is here and getting agitated because you're not at the bar. Sorry."

I looked at Gregg and smiled from my heart for the first time in more than a week.

"I hate when the good things are interrupted by bad things. I need to leave."

He pulled my hand to his lips and kissed each finger separately. "You might be walking away right now, but you're not walking out of my heart. I love you, Lucy. There's something we need to sit down and discuss without distractions. Can we make a date?"

I smiled. "Sure. You say when."

He continued to hold my hand. "I have to make sure Audrey behaves until May seventh. That's her birthday and I'll finally be able to quit watching her like a hawk. How about you see if you can get that night off? I know it's a Ladies' Night but I need to ask you something *very* important--life changing if you will."

His dimple deepened with his smile.

"I'll be there, count on it."

We left the booth and he gave me a quick kiss before leaving the building. My heart was soaring. He'd all but told me what he was going to ask and I knew my answer, yes. Walking to the bar the reality of his statement hit me. He'd said he loved me and was planning to ask me to marry him!

I was smiling from ear to ear when I walked behind Willow to my side of the bar.

"Where've you been?"

The bark of a question turned my smile to a frown.

"Richard, I don't believe that's any of your business."

The thunderous look on his face was frightening. "I'm trying to make sure you're out of harm's way, Lucy. You need to listen to me so you don't get hurt. If you trust me, you'll never cry again."

He turned and stomped out the door.

His statement caught me off guard. When had he seen me cry? I felt a shiver snake down my back. The veiled threat of his statement scared me more than his popping up unannounced. *What is he capable of doing?*

I wasn't able to dwell on my thought as the bar began to fill with state senators after a long night's session. Business would be brisk and tips excellent. I'd filter through the scene with Richard later. Little did I know how many times in the next thirty years I'd rerun that conversation.

Chapter Nineteen

He checked the calendar. Today was the day for which he'd been waiting. Scheduling his time to the last minute before he launched his plans, he was currently soaking in scalding water to rid his body of all the germs he could. He'd bought new clothing to wear for the occasion. All he could hope was she'd appreciate the effort on his part to keep her safe, his Lucy in the Sky with Diamonds. Maybe now she'd see him for what he really was-- her savior.

Rising from the steaming tub, he stepped over the edge and pulled the plug, watching the blood tinged liquid swirl down the drain. Carefully he patted the excess liquid from his body. Three hours still faced him before he left the safety of his home on the mission. His weapon would have to be in the finest form to insure accuracy so he pulled out the cleaning kit and began the careful ritual he performed each time he returned from the firing range. His stomach twinged and he tried to remember the last time he'd eaten.

"Not important. Too excited."

His careful ministrations to the weapon consumed one and a half hours. With the pomp of ritual he dressed. Each item of clothing carefully considered for the importance of this date. One more pass by her apartment and on to his destination. This time tomorrow the world would be different--she would understand and love him for it.

He left his place and ventured to her apartment complex, noting the light still on in her room. She wasn't working tonight? Not a good sign but it was too late to turn back now. He drove the roads to Lucky's not seeing the other cars or traffic lights. Several times he heard honking horns but didn't divert his attention from his task. Slowly he circled the parking lot in search of a spot in the dark. When he was unable to find the exact place he wanted, Richard, The Strange One, parked in the lot across the street and watched the patrons enter the bar. He could make out the thumping of music. *Good, camouflage.*

He pulled the weapon from his glove box and checked the clip, pulling back the slide to ensure a bullet was nestled in the chamber. The car door swung open easily, slamming closed as he set out for his target. He focused on the tavern door, walking blindly across Front Street and up the steps. Opening the heavy entry, he lifted his arm and took a bead on the dark haired bartender.

~ * ~

Shrill ringing interrupted my concentration and made me jump. I glanced at the clock on top of the TV and wrinkled my forehead in consternation. Who was calling me at three in the afternoon? Heck, who was calling me at all?

"Guess answering the phone will solve that riddle. Hello?"

The hesitation on the line threw me. The last thing I needed was a heavy breather.

"Lucy?"

I expelled a breath I didn't realize I'd been holding.

"Hi, Gregg. Today's the day, isn't it? Your problem child will no longer be a problem."

I heard the warm chuckle at the other end of the phone.

"Very true. She's legally twenty-one today so I'm taking her to work with me to help her celebrate. It's the best way I know to keep an eye on her.

"Are you going to make it to the bar tonight?"

I couldn't help the smile that covered my face.

"Oh count on it, Mister. You tossed such a huge hint my direction, I'd call in dead if I had to, but the boss has seen such a change since we talked he figured something *amazing* must be happening. His words. He told me it had better be amazing or he was going to put me on the worst shifts he could find." I chuckled knowing my boss was good for threatening, not good on the follow up part.

"I guess I'll see you there. Probably the best time to come in is about ten thirty. All the tables will be taken, but I'll keep a spot at the bar open for you. I'll be able to take a short break around then."

"Okay, but you'd better pull off something spectacular. You're messing with my livelihood here." I couldn't help the giggle that escaped.

"Lucy?"

"Yes?"

"I love you. Don't ever forget that, now and always. You want spectacular, I'll give you spectacular. How about lights and sirens?"

"I'll take it. And Gregg?"

"Hhhmm?"

"I love you, too."

"Good. It's going to be very important to keep that thought in mind tonight. See you soon, hon."

"Bye." I cradled the phone next to my ear and let the warmth of his velvety voice continue to wrap around me. I checked the clock. I had a few hours before I needed to get ready so I might as well eat. I wasn't sure what sounded good as my stomach was fluttering with excitement butterflies. I fixed something to fill the empty spot and grabbed a book I wanted to finish reading and get back to the library. Even with my excitement, my eyes soon betrayed me and drifted shut.

I woke with a start. The room felt--different and I realized the change was the amount of light *not* coming through the windows. The hands of the clock showed nine thirty.

"Damn it! I'm going to be late. I hate that!" I bolted from the couch, letting the library book tumble from my lap as I tore off my clothes. A quick shower and application of my makeup preceded twenty minutes of trying to get my waist length hair semi-dry. I really needed to put another twenty minutes under the hair dryer for it to be completely done but time seemed to be charging away from me. One last look at myself and I figured I was as put together as I could get. The kitchen clock showed ten twenty.

"Darn it!" I dashed to my car and zipped out of the parking lot. If I was lucky and caught all the lights, I could make it to Lucky's by ten thirty five, a little late but not enough to make a big difference. I started to press down on the accelerator when I heard the whine of a siren.

"No sense getting a ticket." Pulling my foot back, I slowed to the legal speed limit.

A tingling started at the base of my skull and spread through my back. Something odd was happening. I was hearing more sirens, lots more sirens. *There must be a really bad accident on the freeway.* I turned off Portland Road onto Pine Street. The sky lit up with red lights. Glancing in my rear view mirror, I saw a police car accelerating at an unprecedented speed. I moved to the side of the road. Within five seconds another police vehicle screamed past me.

The tingling intensified. *Gregg.* Before another cruiser could appear, I tore away from the curb and raced toward Front Street. As I approached Liberty, I saw the road blocked by more police cars. Streaming in from side streets were several ambulances. The sky was flashing red faster than the strobe lights at the bar. I looked around and pulled into the first parking lot I could find. I jumped from the car and sprinted to Lucky's. As I neared the entrance, strong hands captured me, interrupting my forward motion.

"Sorry, miss, no one is allowed inside."

There were people pouring from inside the building clutching their heads, hands covered in blood.

Panic squeezed at my heart. "GREGG! GREGG!"

I started shouting at the people exiting the bar.

"Ma'am, please. I have to ask you not to yell. Is there someone you're looking to find?"

I turned to the young man in uniform. "Yes. My boyfriend is a bartender here. I need to know if he's okay." I spotted Audrey being escorted by two policemen to a waiting ambulance, blood marking her jeans.

"Officer, I have to find my boyfriend!" I tried to wriggle free of the young patrolman's grip, failing in the attempt.

At that moment, I looked up to see Richard, a policeman on either side of him, in handcuffs being walked to a patrol car. He looked directly at me and smiled.

~ * ~

The trigger compressed so easily, the bartender looking up at the sound of the explosive projectile leaving the barrel. The bullet found its mark and the shocked expression on his face pleased Richard. The feeling of satisfaction egged him on. There were more vermin in this place that needed extermination. Lucy's world couldn't be infested with germs and these creatures were invading her territory. He squeezed the trigger until the bullets failed to leave the barrel. He reached into his pocket and yanked out another clip snapping the shell filled holder into the gun and jerking back the slide to pop another bullet in the chamber.

He stepped further inside the bar and started aiming at the screaming vermin. If they would just die quietly, he could finish his work and head home knowing the world was safe for his Lucy. Click, click, click. The trigger moved with such ease. He stood watching the carnage he was creating. *Vermin. Germs infecting her world. Just like the bartender.* Suddenly, he was staring into the eyes of a man who'd pinned him to the floor. There was pain in his back and chest. He was gulping in air. *Where are all the vermin?* He needed to know. His job wasn't over. The man holding his arms looked angry. He just didn't understand.

"For Lucy."

The man was shaking and squeezing his arms really hard.

The next few minutes were a blur. Richard was lifted from the floor, the gun ripped from his hand, and he was roughly shoved toward the front door.

He needed to be here when she arrived. How would she know what he'd done for her if he didn't get the opportunity to tell her? Richard decided it might be for the best not to make the officers angry. As they pushed him through the door to the outside, he saw her.

Looking at the officer holding his right arm, he smiled. "For Lucy in the Sky with Diamonds."

The policeman shot a wary glance at his partner and shook his head. They led him to the cruiser, driving him to Marion County jail.

~ * ~

I read his lips and crumbled. For Lucy in the Sky with Diamonds. *Oh my god*. What had I done? He warned me. Told me he was going to save me. I buried my face in my hands and allowed the pain to push through. I sobbed until my eyes were swollen and I couldn't push any sound through my throat. When the patrolman was called away to assist in the questioning of witnesses, I trudged blindly to my car. Fleeing the scene, I raced home to the comfort of my apartment. Curiosity ate at me until I turned on the news. Every station was carrying the story of the massacre in Salem, Oregon. Guesstimates of killed and wounded ranged from seven dead and twenty-five wounded to four dead and twenty wounded. The pictures shown on the screen featured the aftermath in graphic detail. Officers from two police agencies were guarding the scene from contamination and thrill seekers.

All I could do was sit on the couch and watch in horror. I couldn't stay in town. There was a knock on my door and I jumped, letting go a scream. I shook from head to toe fearing the Strange One had escaped custody and was back to claim me. Since I'd let whoever was out there know I was inside by screaming, I went to the door and peeked through the spyhole.

Her blonde hair glistened in the lights of the hallway and her eyes were smeared black with mascara.

I opened the door.

"Hi. I know you don't know me but you know... knew my brother, Gregg."

I pulled her into the apartment and showed her to the couch, shutting off the television.

She stuck out her hand. "I'm Audrey."

I grabbed her hand in mine feeling the clamminess of her palms. "I'm Lucy."

She pulled in a deep shuddered breath. "Gregg was acting very strange tonight. He said he had a feeling things were going to be a bit weird so he instructed me to give you this if anything happened." She stuck out her palm on top of which sat a maroon box I recognized from a local jewelry shop.

I shook my head not trying to stem the flow of tears beginning to fall down my cheeks.

"Oh no."

Audrey opened the box. Even in the dimmed light of the room, the solitaire diamond sparkled. "He said to tell you he'd bought this the first time you two talked. He was working up the courage to ask you to marry him. He really loved you, Lucy, really."

My shaking hand snaked out and gently removed the box from her palm.

"I--I--can't. Not after everything that's happened tonight."

Audrey stood up and reached over to stroke my hair. "I have a lifetime full of memories of him. Honor us both and keep it. You would've been a great sister-in-law. I-I have to go. My parents are coming tomorrow to wrap up his affairs and take him home to Spokane."

Moving to the window, she gazed into the darkness, seemingly a million miles from my front room. "I think I'm going to join the Navy and see the world. Goodbye, Lucy."

I tracked her movements as she left through the front door. Popping up from the couch, I locked the door and returned to gaze at the ring in the box.

"Yes, Gregg. I'll marry you. Was there ever any doubt?"

I snapped the box shut and dragged myself to bed. So much had happened in the last twenty-four hours. I was exhausted and deeply in pain. I needed sleep then I needed a new plan.

Taking the maroon box with me, I completed my nightly bedtime routine and crawled beneath the covers. I took the ring from the box and slipped it on my finger. The fit was perfect. I fell asleep wearing my lost future on my hand.

Chapter Twenty

2011

I looked at Cassie's wide eyes and slack jaw.

"Now you know. I'm responsible for the deaths of four people and wounding of twenty."

"Bull. The guy was a nutcase. It had nothing to do with you personally. He just fixated on you. If it hadn't been you, it would have been someone or something else. Trust me on this, Lucy. I've had enough therapy to hang out my own shingle.

"What happened to the Strange One? What did you do? Facts, girlfriend, I need facts."

"Richard White was convicted of four counts of murder and twenty counts of attempted murder. He's in jail in another state for his own safety. The officials were afraid if they kept him here, the survivors or family members of the slain would try to have him killed. Too bad they didn't care that much before he committed the crime.

"Me? I took the money I'd been saving and moved to the California desert outside of Palm Springs. I worked for a while but missed the greenery of the Northwest. When my brother retired back here, I decided it was time to be near family and face my demons. It was then I discovered Lucky's had been torn down and no longer existed. Heck, the whole town of Salem had changed so much I hardly recognized it as the place where I once enjoyed an active social life. Shortly after I came back, you and I met and the rest, as they say, is history."

Cassie rustled herself up from the couch. "Stay here. I'll be back shortly."

I felt a sharking sensation around my calves and looked down into the dark brown orbs of my lab mix. I knelt and pulled her to me burying my face in her fur. She whined and turned to cover my face in doggie kisses.

"Let's go outside."

That was all it took to get the hind end wiggling in happiness. I opened the sliding glass door and stepped into the cool morning with Tessa. She romped across the still wet grass and tore around in circles. Soon she'd discovered a spot that needed her mark and proceeded to do her business. Trotting with her head held high, she came back and sat in front of the sliding door.

"Had enough, have you? Okay, little one."

Cassie had cleaned up and changed her clothes.

"We're going to town."

I frowned. "What for? We have everything we need right here."

She turned a cool stare my direction. "Just get ready."

I grabbed my jacket and purse. "Let's go."

The drive to town was highlighted by the lack of conversation, a very unusual happening. Cassie drove to a parking garage in downtown Salem and she parked the car. I blindly followed her lead. When we stepped into the travel agent's office, my radar went haywire.

"Cassie…"

She ignored me and made a beeline for the desk of the only male agent in the room.

"James."

He'd stood when he saw her.

"Cassie. How very nice to see you. How can I help?"

"This is my friend Lucy. We need reservations in a spa somewhere warm with tropical waters complete with young willing male attendants.

How soon can you arrange it?"

I started to rise from my chair, intent on leaving. "Cassie. I can't take time from work."

"Yes, you can. The time has come for you to heal. Besides, I won't take no for an answer."

"Fine. What about Tessa?"

"I'll arrange for her to be taken care of in a doggie spa while we're gone. Case closed. James?"

He tilted his head and let a small smile creep over his face. "Anywhere particular?"

I shook my head. What was I going to do? Cassie had all the answers. She was right on one hand though; it *was* time for me to start healing.

ABOUT THE AUTHOR

C. L. Kraemer is a wanderer, a way of life started when her father served in the US Marine Corp. She's carried on the tradition seeing most of the continental United States as well as Hawaii and Alaska.

Three contemporary romance novels written under the nom de plume, Celia Cooper, **Old Enough to Know Better, Sun in Sagittarius, Moon in Mazatlan,** and **If Only** were gifts from the writing gods. A fourth novel, **Cats in the Cradle of Civilization,** release date December 2008, written as C. L. Kraemer is her first venture to the mystery genre. *Wings ePress, Inc.* is the publisher of these four offerings.

Healthy Homicide, the October 2008 launch book for a new publishing house, *RoguePhoenixPress,* picks up the torch again in the mystery world. In February 2010, she contributed to two Valentine's Anthologies at *RoguePhoenixPress: A Valentine Anthology,* with a story titled, *Lending Library,* and **A Different Kind of Valentine** with a story titled, *The Prize.*

She has completed the base story, **Dragons Among Us**, August 2010 release by *Rogue Phoenix Press*, for a Dragon Fantasy series. **Dragons Among Eagles**, the second in the Dragons Among series was released in June 2010

Meadows of Gold, another faerie story, was released in **A St Patrick's Day Tale**, March 17, 2011.

Also in the works is a commuter book featuring a motorcycle poker run, **Joker's Wild,** and the third in the dragon series, **Dragons Among the Ice**.

For detailed information, visit her Web sites for background on her books and to follow her travails in writing.

www.celiacooper.com

www.clkraemer.com

www.ingramcontent.com/pod-product-compliance
Lightning Source LLC
Chambersburg PA
CBHW060355180626
46817CB00008B/3018